# GRACE
# FOR GRACE

# GRACE
# FOR GRACE

STORIES | STEVE DE JARNATT

ACRE

CINCINNATI 2020

Acre Books is made possible by the support of the
Robert and Adele Schiff Foundation.

ISBN-13 (pbk) 978-1-946724-30-4
ISBN-13 (ebook) 978-1-946724-31-1

Designed by Barbara Neely Bourgoyne
Cover art: 0194251-CSW © Christopher Swann / BluePlanetArchive.com

The press is based at the University of Cincinnati, Department of
English and Comparative Literature, McMicken Hall, Room 248,
PO Box 210069, Cincinnati, OH, 45221-0069.

Acre Books books may be purchased at a discount for educational use.
For information please email business@acre-books.com.

Dedicated to the memory of my friend Kate Guinzburg.

# CONTENTS

# GRACE
# FOR GRACE

# RUBIAUX RISING

"Never take you back, son, hard as it break my heart," Aunt Cleoma had told Rubiaux. "This the last you come home, we don't break this demon now."

Two weeks ago that was, and since then Rubiaux has sweated away twenty-two pounds of his bedeviled flesh, screaming up in Cleoma's attic, where she nailed him shut. A pot chambre to piss in, another to upchuck the gumbo and crackers he's tried to eat between sieges of nausea. High nineties it's been in the day—just the thing for the bone chills and shivering spasms they both knew came with the territory.

This early morning, as Rubiaux rouses, it is long-dead quiet. Like wads of chawed paper stuck flush back up against eardrums. Just blood rushing nothing in his head. Then blood simmers down, and he can hear gulls squawking on the wind somewhere. He sees gray light squeezing through rippage in the curling tar paper lining the inside of this well-built roof. Wood is bare, creosoted here and there but no paint. He has tried to steal an hour of sleep after an unholy night of ceaseless howl and shredding from the fiercest storm this parish has ever seen. How the roof stayed on was miracle, testament to his late Uncle Zachary's carpentry skill. The extra nail he'd always pound, just to be sure. But that craftsmanship has also imprisoned poor Rubiaux here in dire predicament. All night, as the din of the tempest crescendoed again and again, he thought it surely must be The Rapture. But here he is at dawn—left behind—not risen to heaven.

*Lord, you have tested, and I remain. You grant me new strength, and I will not forget. I will not succumb again to the sorrows of my flesh,* Rubiaux thinks, throat too dry to speak.

Rubiaux has suffered more than one hell. The wounds of war, the subsequent addictions that brought about the necessary cruelty of Cleoma's home-style detox, as well as that Category 5 hurricane last night he still does not even know the name of. But Rubiaux has no idea that another trial—and one far worse than even those—is seeping right this moment through a breach at the base of the 17th Street Canal levee.

Rubiaux has been gone two years and came home with much of him gone. All his ample baby fat. An arm at the elbow. A leg midcalf. There is a large temporary titanium plate across the back of his scalp that is long overdue for replacement. In his most desperate hour, he had tried to pawn it, thinking the metal surely worth some long green. Rubiaux still feels whole most of the time, but not because of that phantom feeling phenomenon they talk about. It was the lush veil of constant OxyContin-crushing and morphine-spiking that kept him unaware of his loss extreme.

Rubiaux was always a kind, self-sacrificing soul. A bit simple, but he had tried to follow a righteous path in life best he could. This justified Aunt Cleoma's repeated troubles to give him one more chance to pull out from his downward spiral. The boy was large for his age, with a fierce dormant temper, but never a boulet. In fact, he beat the local bullies down. Could never stand to see the weak disadvantaged in any way.

When his half-wit cousin Remi went on a two-day binge and got himself hoodwinked by a zealous Marine recruiter, Rubiaux showed up in Remi's stead, taking his name at Camp Lejeune. He bore the burden of boot camp without a solemn peep and, before he could write home, found himself carrying an M60 in a sandy shithole called Al-Najaf.

*The light—the blood and dust—fear's such a human stink here. You just would not believe!* he wrote Aunt Cleoma.

Only two months in country and Rubiaux had run through a barrage of AK and small-arms fire to pull four others from what was left of a Humvee an IED had tunneled a molten hole through. He shook off three sizzling rounds that snapped into his flesh like they were mere bee stings, but a tiny, jagged, crab-shaped piece of shrapnel from the blast was propelled through his skull, deep into some important cleft in his cerebellum. This coma'd him quick as fluid ballooned around his brain. And this was lucky too—he could not feel the catastrophic wounds to his arm and leg from the blast of the second IED. The one meant to kill off those who came in aid.

Rubiaux awoke a month later with slurring speech and a constant liquid fire pumped down his ganglia, searing his tender meridians with such rich raw perpetual agony, he prayed to die a thousand times a day.

Back stateside, his dose-to-pain ratio grew exponentially with his tolerance, and as he had tried to heal in one squalid VA outpatient sty after another, he had twice nearly landed in the brig for narcotic theft. Then, a true absurdity—Rubiaux, a double amputee with severe brain impairment, was declared AWOL. He still was not officially excused from duty, so desperate were they for human fodder to police the chaos wrought over there in New Babylon.

In the attic Rubiaux watches light pour in—dancing dust around, slow and celestial like the Milky Way. His ears improve with a crack-

3

jaw yawn. What's that high-pitched rushing? Those low knocking sounds like bowling heard outside the alley. And that slow, mean rumble. What is coming this way?

A shock wave hits the house like a dozen Peterbilts crashing one after another into the frame. Beams groan, the whole foundation quaking; nails and screws strain to hold their grip, *eeking* like mice as wood and metal mad grapple to hold their forced embrace. A new light shines at the far window, painting the ceiling with golden ripples. Reflection. Water. Water is coming. Water is here.

Rubiaux, who has been through more than anyone should ever have to, tries to remember his comfort song, the one he always hummed in his head on those endless missions, packed sardines inside the furnace of the A2.

"Wingo wheat lariot—" He tries to sing the first notes of the refrain again and again, like a needle that can't hop a scratch-trap groove. "Wingo wheat lariot—comin' for to—comin' for to—comin' to for—for to—to for—" His addled noggin short-circuits. No sweet chariot can take him home today.

Cleoma had gone to town long before the storm. She left in the truck and swore she'd be back before all hell blew with someone who could help pull the nails up from the boarded barriers. But she has not returned.

And where is Remi? How come he never came to visit even once? Rubiaux took bullets meant for the callous lout and even now has not one ounce of anger toward him, only an ache of wondering. Rubiaux looks down through the small hole where Cleoma had pushed up his sodas and daily medicine, doled out strict. He can see angry water rising in the kitchen now, pillaging the house without a hint of mercy. There is no more food in his cooler, and Rubiaux has never been so hungry in his life, but for the first time in two years there is no demon in his veins making him crave sweet oblivion. He looks at what is left of suturing on his arm. He has not looked for months. In the infirmary he could never face the larceny of his limbs. He found that if he made himself numb enough all over, their lack could be forgotten for a spell. Displaced enough from his true axis, he would sometimes reach out with a shadow for a hand, laughing, not connecting to the perversion of his senses—his lying brain believing it was still part of him. He could even snap his ghost fingers and plainly hear the sound. But now he examines the stump all crossed with purpled scars and enjoys the reddened itching of it.

Rubiaux allows himself to face more remembering. The dust of Al-Najaf. The fear and heat. An adrenal thrall boils up quick to that 'lectric shock that keeps that day so vivid in dream and flash-mare. That day—the one he was blasted from being whole. Boys just like him and boys not at all like him. Laughing, braying, praying—all together, tight as one—then the flare of hellfire somewhere and the devil's sneeze of a concussion that ripped apart the Humvee up ahead like it was a Tonka toy.

He remembers the succession of surgeries, one after another, the caduceus vultures coming to pick at his living carcass. "We can try to save the leg…we are unable to save the arm…we have to take a little more…there's another infection, so sorry…just a bit more, son, no other option." He remembers the infinite boredom in between. Most of all he remembers the mind-fucking of Gus Windus, a mean pissant in the next bed who told Rubiaux again and again how he got off easy.

"Ya hear what them fuckers did to Terry Finnell? Strapped that boy down bareback over this big ole metal box chock full o' Baghdad rats. Starved 'em for days, they did. Then they took a blowtorch to the metal. Really lit her up good, roastin' all them rodents. Fuckers ate right up through Terry's belly to get out—path o' least resistance. Poor fucker had to watch 'em all scramble up through his own guts like that guy in the first *Alien* movie."

Rubiaux forever hated rats—since waking as a child to find a small scourge of them nibbling at the blisters on his feet. Finnell's story shivers him again with a flood of harsh memory—then like vermin from an upturned rock, all scatter away to some other dark place. Salt crusts his eyes where tears should be. He has long cried out his life's ration of them. Deep, slow breathing brings him back to the sanctuary of the attic.

What Rubiaux really feels, more than anything, is hunger. Like a panther growling inside him. He has already licked up every crumb he could find up here and is sure he has not missed one. Then, in the wavering light, he sees a vision: the silhouette of something hanging just outside the tiny window at the other end of the attic. *Please*, his mind beseeches no one, *do not let this only be a trick of the eye. That trompe l'oeil would be too cruel, the tempt of it.*

Rubiaux drags himself toward the shadow with all his awkward might, scraping his tissue over the rough floor until he sits beholding it—crimson on crimson in the setting sun—a ripe obese heirloom tomato. Five full inches across, ugly and bulging uneven, the way they were born to be before genetic homogenization rendered their cousins into perfect bland tasteless orbs. A volunteer vine has crawled itself up the side of the house like that beanstalk in the child's tale just to bring this gift to him. Rubiaux plucks the tomato up quick and ponders it as if he were Eve in the Garden. If eating this will change the world, it can only be for the better, and if not, he really doesn't care. His belly rules him at this moment. He can smell the fetid alluvial soil it has grown through—*le terre puant*. He caresses the tension of the tight-stretched circumference, rolls its skin across his cheek, then takes a small bite. The flavor rages through his taste buds, obliterating the stench of the attic. The air outside is no better now, spiced with cesspools, floating gasoline, and the occasional whiff of fresh-rotting death. But this primal taste destroys every bit of it. Rubiaux leaps into its abyss, devouring. Juice and seeds flow down his throat and over his chest. Never has a thing tasted so heavenly. The last of its maroon flesh slides down his parched gullet. He pulls on the vine, careful as can be, and another misshapen wine-colored globe lifts up through the tiny window. He looks at the scratches on the wooden frame where, in his cold-turkey madness, he had kicked the fan out and tried to claw his way through the foot-square hole. He pulls up another, then another—drags the cooler near with his good foot, putting six more magnificent monstrous tomatoes inside.

The creaking of the whole house suddenly amplifies as the leveled wash begins to seep upward through the cracks and holes in the kitchen *plafonnage*. Like a string of dirty pearls, a dozen wet mice come pouring up ahead of filthy gray water that makes separate little flows all over, merging like quicksilver into greater water and rising still.

Rubiaux stacks three large travel cases in this corner near the window. He crawls up, leaving him not even a foot to the tarpaper ceiling when he sits upright. The water rises and rises quick, inch by living inch.

The sun is sinking fast. Rubiaux realizes he may drown here in darkness—far from his choice of leaving this life. He curls up against the corner. There is a long ledge, a foot wide, high up in the rafters where he can put the cooler and stretch out his good leg. He eats another tomato, savoring every morsel, and he prays to keep the rising at bay. Prays the way all have done in The Easy and the bayous forever. Those prayers had always seemed answered, peril postponed till another day as each storm would somehow graze away from them, sparing their special voluptuous lives. Till now.

Distant shouting melts with the whistling of the breeze through the cracks. Rubiaux closes his eyes before the light is gone so he can remember it all—then wills himself to sleep.

Rubiaux awakes out of time, in pitch darkness. He scratches his leg where it isn't with his hand that is not there. The water is now up over the stacked supports, soaking him a good inch. But it has stopped. Prayer has worked, if only partly. But there is something new in the darkness now—breathing, movement. Others. He keeps his own breath steady, feigning slumber, waiting for light to grow in the east.

When he slowly opens his eyes again an hour later, he sees them—the unholy menagerie. All down the ledge, crowded near him in awkward proximity, are a large kingsnake, two smaller water snakes, four fat nutria, a half-drowned feral cat with two shivering kittens, three pitiful brown rabbits, a soggy raccoon, a dozen Norwegian rats, a clot of huddled mice, along with a teeming mess of spiders, beetles, centipedes, and such. His eyes dart. Theirs do too. All seem to breathe in some strange unison. Waiting a move. Nobody is eating anybody this morning. They share the same fear and confusion—fellow orphans in the storm.

Rubiaux ever so slowly lifts the brim of the cooler. He offers an heirloom to the kingsnake, which twists itself back into a tighter coil. He rolls it down the rafter toward the nutria, who clutch it up, nibbling through the skin. He tosses another down the ledge toward the rats, but it rolls askew, off into the water, bobbing there in shame. The next one barrels right into the rodents, who share it with the rabbits till the coon takes it away from the both of them. There is a peace here he never thought possible on this Earth. Wild beasts together, the lion and the lamb—a living Bible story of some lost Eden.

Then—another mountain of liquid slams into the house, ending this bliss. The nutria fall into the water and paddle off. The structure has slipped fully off the foundation and is splaying itself down into the weak muddied ground. Whether the water is rising or the house is sinking, it matters not—in minutes Rubiaux will surely drown.

The sound of a Sikorsky is heard, the circular clicking hovering not far off. Rubiaux again tries to claw at the hole of the window, tearing fingernails off, but this hole will never get bigger. Time to die with snakes and rats, his newfound friends.

Rubiaux takes comfort in the knowledge that at least he is clean, his mind clear—and he is ready to meet his Maker.

Looping his belt around his throat, Rubiaux secures it up over a two-by-four, cinching it tight across his Adam's apple. He wishes not to go by drowning, having nearly done so twice in life. In death he chooses hanging, which someone once told him is fairly quick, and you might even get a raging bone on as you blinded out in a red gruesome rush.

Just before giving himself to gravity, he notices warping patterns of golden light dancing around the roof. This baffles him. He tries to see it straight on, but it keeps moving, always off to his periphery again. Then he realizes the sun is hitting the shiny curved titanium plate on the side of his head. This makes Rubiaux laugh. He squints till it looks to him exactly like an angel floating free above his shoulder. Then, in a flash, he knows what he must do. As if the angel told him.

It takes some prying, tearing the rest of his fingernails to get it loose. Then, using a rusty nail for leverage, he stuffs it up under a gap between the plate and the tender, fibrous growth of his scalp and yanks hard as he can. It comes clean off, falling into the water, gleaming there like a lure. He snatches it up before it fades from view, shaking off the droplets, then trains the convex side sunward, compounding the rays into a blinding hot spot on the roof. In seconds tarpaper bursts flame, coughing out thick black hellfire smoke. The rest of his natural guests leave as fast as they can scurry, slither, or hop away. Rubiaux feels bad about this and prays safe passage for them all, even the rats.

When the smoke hugging the ceiling gets too thick, he pulls the cooler down over his head and drops into the water with the brim submerged around him. He holds there as long as he can, safe in the air pocket. Something sinister in the water brushes between his thighs, then comes back to nibble at his suturing. Oxygen is used up quickly, and he weakens, in danger of not having the strength to lift the cooler away, but then shoves with all he has left and sees there is now a three-foot hole in the roof, encircled with red flame. Through it he can see a helicopter lowering down through the plumes. Rubiaux flashes the angel glint up toward the cockpit window, and the behemoth hovers closer, clearing smoke from the attic.

The pilot rubs his eyes several times, not sure of what he is seeing.

On the side of the roof, two snakes are stretched out over each other, forming a perfect cross on the burning roof.

This craft is already full up, but one of the bone-tired Coast Guard heroes who have labored valiantly with no rest descends down in a basket, pulling Rubiaux aboard, strapping them together. They rise up, flying Rubiaux low over one submerged ward after another—to the heart of the drowned Crescent City. Passing over gas fires, families wading chest-high, looters floating plasma televisions, dogs in trees, and so many other sights Rubiaux thought he would never see.

As they set him down on the overpass near the Dome with the huddled bunches of others, Rubiaux knows his suffering is finally over. Help and comfort will surely be coming soon.

# MULLIGAN

They are drawn now from all directions—families down to their last drop of hope, coming through the gauntlet of a gathering storm, to the dead center of America. They have until midnight to cross the border here in The Cornhusker State, before the music stops.

Arabelle Tunney drives a rusted Ford camper exactly the posted limit, heading east out on Highway 70—the comforting drone of engine and wind pierced by a shrill wave of young laughter.

"Simmer down, back there, simmer down!" she shouts to her children in the rear.

Arabelle buried her husband Earl under the turnips out in the truck patch late Tuesday night. His kidneys gave out at long last. Earl had a well-documented history of renal trouble, but the Warfarin-laced stews she fed him the last few days probably helped the reaper do his work.

The bastard Earl kept Arabelle knocked up without mercy, seeding her womb/his "property" with seven children in six years. Because the Lord told him to. She hid away inside her ample girth—only her ornery toes would betray feelings sometimes, making the sounds of animals scuffling under a rug, clicking and squirming down in the fortress of her hard shoes.

She's leaving hell back in The Beehive State, en route to the high plains of freedom and a second chance at everything. It's not just mouths to feed with no option but charity that has her in distress; it's the six-year sum of all that's been inflicted on a child bride thrown into such cruel arrangement. Arabelle longs to know so much: Google, travel, and tender love. But she's known only Pampers, breast-feeding, and the sting of a backhand slap.

Five girls and two boys. At least now the eldest, Dora, can help some with the toddlers. These angels of hers should bring joy, but they reflect only some blank, engulfing sorrow. Sometimes when Arabelle looks their way, they have no faces. Sometimes their voices scree like wounded birds, and their eyes swirl like fun-house pinwheels. She craves a week of narcotic sleep, maybe a year of it—to not, for god-damn once, have something leeching off her blood, her milk, her time.

The children look out windows greased with nose prints, searching the lateral flow of countryside for white horses and old barns, a contest to pass the time. As they sing an old hymn, their off-key harmonies reach deep into Arabelle's brain and begin to turn the red-hot screws again.

🕊

Ned Laporte drives his yellow Saab north from The Land Of Enchant-ment. No need to rush, he left with time to kill. Noise cancellation headphones protrude from either side of his narrow, shiny pate. As tears crust on his cheeks, Ned smiles at the road ahead, spinning the crackling dial through a spectrum of fading stations. The confluence of three major fronts is birthing a statewide electrical storm. Light-ning flashes somewhere, and speckles of a drought-ending rain begin to pelt evenly across a thousand acres. Petrichor sublime—air spiced with a bouquet of fresh-dampened soil.

Ned's seven-year-old son, Byrd, squirms, strapped in a booster seat in back, face eclipsed by a bowl of black hair, hanging wet. The boy's hands are tethered together, on each a soft leather mitt. He wears goggles to save his eyes from mashing; a bike helmet protects his head, bobbing like a sports souvenir. Byrd screams at the top of his lungs.

"You know I can't hear you when I have these on. And you know your throat will bleed when you yell like that," father calmly shouts to son. Ned beholds the perpetual fidget his boy is stricken with. He has always done the calm, correct thing with Byrd. Until this day. The boy's tantrum melts to a passive slouch, and his eyes meet Ned's in the rearview. A precious thing, such connection.

"It's not your fault," says Ned, and Byrd looks away.

Ned met his wife Lenore through Mensa personals, and it seemed perfect, two sensible, solvent academics on the fast track to tenure. Lenore's fragile beauty was beyond any the average-looking Ned could ever really hope for, yet after two months there she was, agreeing to be his wife. The hooks went deep.

They both had a great wish for children, which proved difficult, then impossible. In their third year of marriage, after enduring a lengthy and humiliating process, they were finally blessed with a year-old orphan from Moldova. They kept his given, Bogdan, meaning *gift of God*—nicked that down to Bog, then switched to Byrd for the way he would sometimes tilt his head back begging food.

All babies cry, but Byrd never stopped. They knew, at the moment of his first seizure, it would not be the bliss of rearing they'd imagined.

"He's defective," Lenore had said.

"He's our son," he'd told her.

Ned stayed home with Byrd, putting his career on hold to maintain the constant nurturing the difficult boy required as Lenore traveled more and more on the university lecture circuit. She withdrew, seldom even touching the child. For years the couple maintained the façade of what was expected of decent people, but in the end the price for Ned was this—Lenore or Byrd. He still cannot believe the choice his heart is making.

Byrd lifts a plastic bottle from his lap, holding it with force between the awkward mitts. He sucks on the teat of it until a mouthful is ready, then spits the soymilk concoction across the back of his father's head. Ned does not flinch. He was expecting this. White glop swirled with blood hangs a moment, then slips down his neck across an already caked and drying mess. Byrd laughs, and growing louder, the sound turns back into a scream.

Coach Ike Pisapia floors his Dodge Ram balls out, racing up from The Lone Star State to beat the deadline. A large man, slumped in pain—his jaw tight and bothered, blue eyes red and watering. Mack and Jack, his corpulent fourteen-year-old twins are ensconced in the quad cab playing World of Warcraft, one of many games that have usurped their young lives.

"We hungry yet?" Coach asks, and as if to answer *Nope, we're fine*, Mack rattles a half bag of Cheetos, not bothering to look up.

Coach had been an always-picked-last chubby teen, just like them, but he willed himself into a lettered athlete at Texas A&M. The summer after high school graduation he became a new boy, eating only raw eggs and vegetables and doing his own killer two-a-days. He read *The Power of Positive Thinking* endlessly, then walked on for varsity football with a different body and a ferocious new spirit, making special teams squad freshman year.

Coach has taken the twins to athletic contests since they could walk and tried to fuel them with healthy food and dreams. He's played tapes of Larry Bird, Billy Mills, and a hundred others, encouraging them to choose whatever sport they wish, as long as they try to bust their ass at something. Anything. But Mack and Jack are bereft of will-power—all they do is gorge on processed crap, twitch their thumbs to kill imaginary monsters, shit, sleep, masturbate, and do it all again, day after day.

Last year Coach arranged to take the boys to a Galveston morgue. Four dead bangers on the slabs after a gang shoot-out.

"You look long and hard at these fools," Coach told them. "Full of life yesterday, now they all torn up with their purple guts leakin' out. This is your cost of real violence."

The twins seemed mildly bored with the corpses, only muttered that the bodies smelled then went back to finger-fucking their little boxes.

Why are his little men so damn soft—so lost? That estrogen in all the food the magazines talk about? Because he spared the razor strap his daddy used to mold him? Has he failed them with kindness, or is there something more? Does he blame them for breaking her open, for taking his one true love away? Marie and Coach were an in-separable couple, never a day apart. If she hadn't made that road trip with him—miles from nowhere on the way back from league quar-terfinals, her breech could have been attended to, so it's as much on Coach's soul what happened that night.

Loose skin hangs from sinew around a constellation of bruises where he keeps an IV flowing. He has only months left, the doctors say. He wants to live it full and, if he can, get another liver and last a little more. Coach knows he's a stone-cold shit weasel for what he is set to do, but he's claiming his own precious time—he can do no more as a bad father.

❦

Every state has its Haven law, granting license to leave an unwanted child at any hospital, law enforcement office, or fire station. Thirty days is par for the course, up to a year in The Flickertail State. But here in Nebraska, the last to enact, the age was somehow set at seventeen,

and the gesture of mercy has spawned a fiasco of unintended consequence, deluging the social service network with an overflow of
humanity, or lack thereof. Lawmakers toil in special session in Lincoln
tonight, called back from fishing trips and mistress trysts to undo
the gaffe they signed into law only months ago. Tomorrow it comes
to an end.

While Omaha, Lincoln, and the east have borne the brunt, out in
southwest Nebraska they've been ill-prepared at best for any on-
slaught of urchins. The abandoned youth in these outskirt counties
from Red Willow to Keith have been rounded up and temporarily cor-
ralled at the Sleepee Teepee Motor Court—a kitschy roadside wonder
boarded up for years and scaly with pentimento, just a stone's throw
from the County Fire Station on the 61. The rooms reek of Lysol and
old bodily fluids, and bedbugs lurk in half the mattresses—so eleven
youngsters run wild outside, playing games until the evening comes,
milking the gift of an Indian summer. They camp out in the castles
and volcanoes on what's left of a once glorious miniature golf course,
now rotting in the elements behind the motel.

Yesterday Del Manners, an apprentice fireman from the station,
was helping out. He reattached a makeshift blade to a pint-sized
windmill as a hubbub of youthful noise orbited around him. Shirley
Hempstead, the veteran DHHS liaison sent out by the state, handed
him another section of baling wire and a pair of needle-nose.

"You hear about that couple from Saginaw flew into Eppley last
week to dump eight kids with the TSA?" Del asked, and she clucked a
tongue. "Drew straws—then took just one back home again."

"Headin' up to the Sand Hills tonight," she said, walking a circle
around him. "Five more come down from the Dakotas, 'nother meth
family. Back tomorrow. Soon as the governor signs, I'm off to Lincoln
with the load. Booked a charter; should be en route about now. Sure
you're ok to spell me?"

"We thawed our freezers. Least none goes hungry," Del said, then
stepped down and stood awkwardly in front of her. "About last night—"

"You're married, Del. And I'm not quite divorced."

"Another time, then."

"Was just the once."

Del held the sheepish pout of a chastised pet, whimpering for a head pat. The older Shirley sighed, scratching a ruddy splotch on the back of her calf, then something fragile shattered nearby and broke their moment too.

"Augie!" Shirley shouted over at a grimy towhead, buck-naked but for his mismatched cowboy boots. He stood atop a giant tire leaned up against the building—smashing in motel windows with a length of pipe, trying to sing like T-Pain. She hurried off to disarm and dress the little demon, and Del moved on to brace up a lighthouse that was tilting like the Tower of Pisa.

You could quickly see reasons for some being given up, Del thought. Like Augie from The Show Me State—put on the train to Lincoln, but kicked off at McCook. He tore holy hell out of all things Amtrak, biting and kicking whatever was in his path. Damn near feral.

Some broke your heart. A tiny girl, Xiang Lee, the product of a night of errant groping between code lemmings out in The Golden State. Her father was yanked back to Bangalore when his H-1B expired. Her mom, a programmer from South China, kept the child mainly in the bathroom until she was three, slept her in the tub, afraid to let another soul know she even walked the earth. Two ancient lineages should surely mix well, but by some curse of the helix, Xiang was born with claw-like appendages—cursed worse to be unloved. When the mom got wind of the new Nebraska law, she drove all night, dumped her daughter with the Chase County Sheriff's Office in Imperial, and hightailed it back to Guangzhou. Xiang has been near invisible at the Sleepee Teepee, hiding wherever she can.

Wild tantrums were contagious for a time. The madness of sudden change. But bled of tears and sleep, the tykes have found a strange solace and community—making up the way of the world for themselves.

Still in early training as a ladder-truck driver, Del would love to have a manual to help guide him. He makes sure the children are warm and well fed, and keeps them occupied with hand-me-down toys, but generally fails to answer the impossible questions of where their parents have gone. Tomorrow they'll be packed off back east, to disappear into the cold maw of the foster care system.

🐦

Molly Swisher twists the key in an old Crown Coach school bus, sixty miles over the border in The Centennial State. She sips Irish joe from a paper cup, flints a butt she found left in the ashtray. Molly bought the pink slip with twelve hundred dollars won at craps a year ago. The bus sits mainly in the driveway of her "dream home," a four bedroom in the mid 300s, part of a new development tract gone belly up. The engine mule kicks, finally churning over, choking out a black fart of oily wind.

"Atta girl, Delilah." She pats the blistered dash of the yellow beast.

Molly checks her morning face in the pull-down mirror—the sun-worked skin just like her mother's, teeth she rarely shows until she knows you well, mid-thirties mistook for late-forties more often than not. She was all set to drive for the new school district here, but like everything in this mirage community, the job was a promise unkept. She wills the vehicle into gear, and it rolls off down the way.

Molly has pulled her own weight in this world since being run off a Pentecostal home just shy of fifteen back in The Tar Heel State. Bus driver was to be her latest incarnation for plying a trade—on a long and varied list including bass player in an L7 tribute band and crewing in Alaska during salmon roe season. She's managed to book a few field trips up to Rushmore for some smaller schools in the area, but it's been piecemeal at best. She's been hired to transport the Haven law children from the Sleepee Teepee back to Lincoln, some on to Omaha and God knows where.

To miscarry as many times as Molly and hear of such abandonment made her come half unglued. "How the hell could anyone give up their own flesh?" she'd asked, but clammed up quick and took the job.

She squints out across the ruby dawn above her aborted cul-de-sac as the bus lumbers down a blank avenue. Only thirty-six of the planned six hundred homes were ever built; the rest of the lots lie fallow, along curbed streets and sidewalks gently curving nowhere.

Molly bought here nothing down—in on the ground floor of a good thing, roots for once, a place to raise family. She enjoyed pretending it was a cabin in the woods when she first moved in, helping the workers complete the interiors. The day their pay was stiffed again, the drywalleros shoved the sheetrock from the truck to rot in a ditch, leaving her with skeleton walls and dangling wires where appliances should be. What had been a din of round-the-clock construction fell to silence. The developer's phones rang dead. She's four months in arrears on her albatross loan, living off the leavings of other abandoned homes, but Molly has steeled herself to make a stand here, homesteading in the half-formed landscape of the modern dream.

The bus chugs on through the pedestrian square, where the theater and state-of-the-art gym were to be, coming upon a slumbering herd of buffalo blocking the way. They must not have got the memo—this is no longer open range. Molly eases through them, heading east through the last shoulders of the Rockies toward the Nebraska state line.

🐦

Toes cramped and aching, Arabelle shifts her heel up to the pedal, keeping a steady sixty-five. She reaches deep in her bag for another clot of yellow diet pills, long past expiration. You can't change a mind so easy if you keep yourself in motion. If you slow or stop, you might wake up from one nightmare into another—his breath upon you—a magazine rolled and ready—his ghost screaming why?

Arabelle lowers the window and sniffs the metal tang of ozone, remembering electric motors and fish tanks her daddy kept. The brood sleeps soundly in back as the distant sky begins to crack open. In the hush between thunders, she listens as seven little out-of-phase snores come gently into alignment, holding unison for several magic seconds.

Arabelle can feel a world of change just around the corner. Her hamster wheel is finally coming to a stop. The cage door will open soon, and she can slip out and hide somewhere.

✦

Byrd screams for another twenty miles, seizes up, and passes out. Ned pulls to the shoulder and cleans them both as best he can, resecuring the boy in the passenger seat. Byrd has calmed upon waking, happy to be riding shotgun. He hangs his face out in the wind, canine style. This late afternoon a massive static charge sizzles above the parched rolling hills, and Byrd seems touched by it, as if his nervous system craves some osmosis of the amperage building.

"We're driving over the world's biggest aquifer—the Ogallala. It stretches from South Dakota all down through the panhandle to the caves of Carlsbad. Been so depleted by drought and irrigation, it was on the brink. Quite the godsend, this rain. The storm will really help replenish."

Byrd nibbles a corndog with the stick removed as they motor through The Sunflower State. The first flash of lightning spider-cracks the sky—singeing their retinas, leaving bright ghosts drifting through their mind's eyes. Ned begins to count until the thunder comes.

"Ten miles off," he says as a low rumble bowls across the land. "Looks like they jolt down from the sky to earth, but actually it's the reverse. Too quick for the eye to see."

"Tin mi," mimics the boy who rarely speaks, turning to his father with wonder in his eyes.

"What, son?"

"Amm lectreec!"

For the first time in a hundred miles, Ned's PDA finds a network out in the troubled ethers. He texts Lenore, who swore she would fly back from The Garden State, meet them for this last goodbye, .

*You enroute?*

*Plane delayed. Nothing I could do. Is it over?*

*It?*

*You know what I mean.*

*Trips done Byrd a world of good. You wont believe it.*

*Thats great. I'm glad. Does not factor in.*

*Lenore you have to see him.*

He waits for a reply, but there is nothing more to come.

Ned agreed to follow Lenore to her new department head position at Rutgers. A clean start—they would cut their old friends off, make new ones, and never mention any son. There was a narrow window of opportunity, and it was a chance to save them. Lenore could be persuasive.

A thousand jagged bolts begin to scratch the horizon, and Ned times the lag of every thunderclap. Tumbleweeds wheel in the staccato brightness, and he and Byrd witness the mad dash of jackrabbits and nimble fowl darting every which way through the chaparral. It seems every able creature is stampeding across Kansas, like lemmings.

Coach stops to swallow medicines, and pills spill from his trembling hand. The twins remain oblivious, glued to Level 70, the tinny score from their games twinkling whenever things rumble quiet. He's made a long list, nothing on it sports related. Coach is done with wholesome life lessons and personal growth. He seeks some new wanton path, a hedonistic spree. He'll change his name, keep driving, and never look back. The Dodge Ram has 54,000 miles. He hopes to pass 200,000 before he dies.

The next coruscation erupts into a roiling ball of angry blue and yellow light, miles away in the low northern sky. The expected thunder does not peal, but instead comes the slap of a significant shock wave. Devil smoke and mad flickering climb heavenward as more explosions nearly blind the eye.

As the yellow bus coasts down onto the endless expanse of the High Plains, Molly catches glimpses of the same disturbing light show off to the east. She ponders if it's even worth the drive back to her development after the job. She could sell the bus, take what she gets, and look for something out in Omaha. In the spring she could work concessions at the College World Series and root for some scrappy team. Might be a good life there.

*Walk away! Abandon your mortgage!* Molly heard a man on TV say. Her ex, Tim Gentry, would surely hate such a coward's thought. One should make good on a hard promise, even if it was cajoled with brokers' lies. *You gave your word, and your word is your bond*, he'd say. Quite a thing to be judged so harshly by a man you met in a prison chat room, but Tim was sent up for shooting at the Assessor, claiming they've never had the right to tax—so he holds himself above a lot of things.

Molly had known since she was a little girl it was her destiny to be a good mother, and she and Tim tried hard each conjugal they allowed. Every time, it took—just like that, the strip turned blue; there would be the heartbeat, then the snowy shape. First two were boys, Henry and Louis. Named for kings. But the template of creation was not within her, and each perished before the third trimester. Had it been a jinx to have given names? The next child was left without, just in case.

Tim escaped his work farm down in The Pelican State, stole a car and drove north to be there for the birth of this child, the only one to make it out into the light. The doctor knew from the stillness and the empty heft—it was only so much organic matter now, not anyone's daughter. Tim got another six years tacked on and cut her off. He wanted someone who'd breed his legacy, and he moved on, trolling the incarceration chats again.

A dull chime rings deep within her good ear, pressure built from altitude and barometric drop. Atmospheric machinations are afoot, and Molly can feel a shadow cross the land. She drives on—smack dab into the eye of it all.

❧

Across the Nebraska state line Ned crests a knoll, heading toward the lights of the next small town—Byrd peaceful in seizureless sleep. Ned observes the verdant hue of the furious cluster of cumulonimbi boiling low above them. Far off like gunfire something comes closing fast—crack-crack-crack—so loud it shakes bones. Something shatters, then another, then too many to count. Ned cranks up the wavering classical station to drown the frightful sound, only making it seem some blasting movie trailer. The windshield gets bashed again and again, and he pulls the Saab beneath a narrow train trestle for some small cover. Byrd wakes, showing not a shred of fear, and Ned hugs him, praying a funnel hasn't formed that could snatch them skyward at any second.

As the din weakens, Ned realizes it's only the ass end of the maelstrom, voiding its burden in fist-sized shards of hail. Out in the headlights, as far as they can see, glass meteors streak and burst to pieces. Some bounce and dance themselves to a stop. Ned and Byrd grin ear to ear, rapt in transcendental awe—then the heavenly spigot shuts off as suddenly as it opened, leaving the road crystal-strewn, a faint crackling all around them.

❧

Coach pulls over outside the County Firehouse on Highway 61 as sirens scream up to pitch inside.

"Pretty damn cool, huh?" he says, getting out to assess his cratered hood. "Like being bombarded out in the asteroid belt in your starcraft or something." The twins exchange an eye-roll glance.

Firemen scramble to pull on gear and ready engines as Del Manners comes running up the road from the Sleepee Teepee, riled and winded. He's the last to dress and climb aboard as trucks race off toward the violent light in the next county, where a grain silo has been struck, sparking an explosion of sugar beet dust and setting off a daisy chain of mayhem.

As sirens fade, Arabelle parks the camper opposite the firehouse, slapping her numb-dead leg to come halfway back to feeling. She makes sure each youngster has their bundled clothes as the brood disembarks, leading them like ducklings toward the open door.

*We got hellacious engulfment out here—worse than Scottsbluff. Three dead and God knows how many set to join 'em. Gonna need every able man or gal out here—ten more silos on the verge,* barks a harried voice from the station squawk box.

The building is empty, hanging thick with diesel as Arabelle dispenses quarters for the soda machines in the back, then hurries off toward the camper.

"I'll go get us more change," she calls out.

Arabelle opens the driver's door, glancing back for one last look at her children, who open drinks and explore the world around them. Something shifts above, and before she can even know it, her hand has reached out by reflex and caught a hailstone tumbling from the roof.

Driving west, Arabelle guns the camper up to eighty-five—wild at last. She licks the frozen orb as if it were a popsicle.

🐦

Sirens Doppler past the motor court, and children come out to watch the red beacons whip through twilight. The little demon Augie blinks at the distant boiling sky, unwrapping his king-size Kit Kat bar as the others collect around him. It would be in his nature to gobble it all just to spite them, but this time he hands a chunk of it to the larger boy he beat down yesterday, then breaks the rest in two, then in two again and again and gives up all the pieces. As if he's heard a beckoning, Augie sets off in a brisk walk toward the firehouse a quarter mile away. The others follow him like he is Moses leading them into the desert.

Ned, cruising past, sees the march of children. Byrd waves, and some wave back.

❧

"Last pit stop for a long patch now," Coach tells his boys as they walk into the mouth of the firehouse.

"Where're we goin', anyhow?" one of his boys mumbles.

"Don't know, son, but when we get there, I guess we will."

The twins disappear into the head, and Coach retreats, avoiding the eyes of Arabelle's curious tots, as if one look from them might skewer him like a spear. Near the door, he hustles to a wastebasket, urping out his lunch. He undulates and makes a wounded sound until there is nothing left but clear liquid. Dora stands in front of him as he pulls his head away. She offers him a napkin and her Cherry Coke. He takes the napkin, then hurries back to his truck—his life—his death.

❧

Molly parks Delilah at the Sleepee Teepee. No one answers her knocking on any of the doors. Shirley from DHHS was to meet Molly here to help chaperone the forsaken back to Lincoln, but a washed-out bridge in the Sand Hills has left her stranded in the north.

Molly reads a framed article on the wall about an old fort that once stood on these same grounds. When smallpox decimated the local Pawnee, their warpath returned the favor, leaving the surviving sodbusters holed up there, nearly starved out during a long winter's siege. Fragments of families stitched themselves together into new bloodlines, and those fresh clans bullheaded on after the peace was made, at least until the fort and everything around it got flattened by a tornado, the rebuilding abandoned the next year during a locust plague.

"Times ain't tough today, no matter what they tell you," she mutters to no one.

Walking around the bleached Astroturf and peeling iconic structures out back, Molly drifts toward a feeble cry on the breeze, finding tiny Xiang Lee weeping inside a giant conch shell of crumpled fiberglass. She has woken from a dream to find herself alone. Molly swaddles the girl in a coat and carries her to the bus. Xiang Lee tries to hide her clawed hands, but Molly makes a point of kissing each of them.

"You're a mermaid, aren't you? Oh, yes you are," Molly says, and Xiang gives up the sliver of a smile.

Ned lays a frayed woolen blanket across the firehouse kitchen table, chock full of hailstones. He removes the mitts from Byrd so he might feel the frigid rough perfection of them.

"Three of the largest hailstones on record fell right here in southwest Nebraska," he tells the children. "It's a vortex for such things."

Dora and the rest of Arabelle's brood come round as if Ned were Mr. Wizard, watching him crack the largest one in two.

"See the layers, like an onion. To make one of these little devils, a tiny speck—just a kernel of dirty nothingness—must get sucked into the updraft of a powerful thunderhead. More water freezes around the speck of graupel at the top of the angry cloud. It's buffeted around up there, but gets so heavy it falls back down to earth, melting all the way from friction, gathering more dust and water, then rising and falling, again and again."

The children each take one to hold. Some stretch tongues to taste the residue of storm still imbedded in the ice. Dora sneaks three cold balls into her pockets, to save for later.

"You could call them the pearls of the sky," says Ned.

A water-stone crumbles to mush in Byrd's hand. He laughs, and this time it does not turn to scream. As he squashes another one down to sleet, Arabelle's young boys do the same. Molly Swisher walks in carrying Xiang and gravitates to Ned, the only adult in sight.

"You in charge here?" she asks.

"They all ran off to put out a grain silo fire, I think," he tells her as Augie and the others from the motel run over, joining in the hail ball crushfest.

"You're not with Health and Human? I'm supposed to drive some kids back east tomorrow."

"We—my son and I—we were just driving past. Came in to get out of the storm," Ned says as Molly looks at all the children, on the cusp of tears.

"You heard about this—this law? What they let you do here?"

"I heard," says Ned, blushing halfway to crimson.

"Fuckers oughta all be strung up by their balls. Tits too. Man and wife! You're spittin' right in God's eye, giving up your own," she whispers.

"Yes, they should. Bastards," he whispers back.

🐦

In a booth at a greasy spoon in the next town, Arabelle pours gravy across the food mountain on her plate, counting out the dollars to her name as Coach Pisapia devours his second Monte Cristo sandwich at the counter. Their eyes meet and, with no reason not to, stay locked a moment. If he squints, she could be the spitting image of his young Marie. He twitches a good minute before getting up the gumption.

"Hey over there—how's that gravy, anyway?" Coach asks Arabelle.

"Well, I make better from scratch."

"You cook, then?"

"All the time."

"For who?"

Arabelle's lowers her gaze. "Just myself now."

"Sounds a little lonely."

They kill two bottles of Mateus and a whole pecan pie. Coach picks up both checks, and they ride east in his hail-dented Dodge, leaving her camper on the shoulder, Earl's loaded Colt under the seat.

"Think you ever might want kids?" he asks her down the road a ways.

"Not if you paid me a million in gold," she replies, unlacing her well-worn boots and tossing them out the window. Coach smiles, knowing whatever time left in this life, it will be better than before.

Children squeal and tease, scuff knees and pee their pants on into the night. More reports from the silo explosions pour in—word that a young ladder-truck driver was paralyzed by flying debris, with triage underway for six more wounded.

Byrd, who has always avoided those his age, joins the play—Hide and Seek and Kick the Can. When the batteries die in their game devices, Mack and Jack watch the others awhile, then jump in as well, telling Xiang Lee she has awesome weaponry for hands and picking her for their side in King of the Hill. Later, with Molly and Ned spotting down below, the larger children take turns sliding down the pole.

"Kids say the motel up there has the chiggers somethin' fierce, so maybe best we all stick around here tonight," Molly tells Ned.

The cupboards are raided, and they make a mulligan stew to remember, then children begin to wilt like flowers—tucked, two by two, into the firehouse bunks.

"Think these firemen'd miss some Costco cans if I took a few?" Molly asks Ned.

"If they did, they'd get over it."

"Wards of the state now."

"Breaks your heart."

28

"Boys Town'll take in some. Foster for the rest, and that's both a good thing and a bad. But every last one scarred for sure."

"Helluva thing."

Molly falls asleep with her head in Ned's lap. When a text from Lenore comes in at 5 a.m., he pries the batteries from the device and without looking gently drops it in the trash.

# EGGTOOTH

I pull my rickety wagon the five blocks from the Motor Inn before sunup. Uncle Travis and Aunt Ivy were still snoring in the other bed as I snuck out. I worry dawn's chill might do Suzie harm, but least it keeps her curled tight in the tool chest for now. I will leave it all at school when it's done. When it's over I will set her free.

There I see it now, peeking through the trees—the special place that took me in and showed me the whole wide world. Today I show them where I come from and they will not look away. They will know me a whole lot better when it's done.

As I cross the playground, my angry insides pull me to the commode. Always feel so set to go but never can on a day of *The Proving*. Sitting here in this cold stall I hear them coming in behind me—beauties they think they are, but harpies for sure if they don't see the light. They speak of me like I weren't here, though they know just exactly where I sit.

"That little hillbilly gonna show and tell today?" says one.

"If creepy carrot-top bit you with that rotten snaggle of hers, you'd need the rabies shots for sure," says another.

I let this all roll on off of me like duckwater. The girl in the next stall is talking to her food—saying goodbye to the breakfast she just ate as she upchucks it all in the bowl. She has napkins and gargle juice handy, as if it's a common thing to do. And I am the strange one here, they say.

They finally leave me be. In the mirror I see me. Nothing special, but not so awful neither. In photos sometimes I see what they all talk about, frozen in a flash—a cross-eyed child awash with too much freckling, the bumpity paste of skin, orangey rag-doll hair, and a twisted Bucky Beaver grin. Can't help myself to smile. I walk in constant joy. I smile in my sleep. My eyes smile. They say it takes you twenty-six different face muscles to smile. But not me—I got one permanent. Takes me muscles not to.

Carlton Day School put me on scholarship here because of my figuring on the state test. Made me take a dozen more when nobody believed the first scores. They found I can riddle out computations any which way you want. My kin always knew. Born this way. Numbers have always been my friends. I can see them somehow where they hide, and they talk to me, showing the strings between them and the easy ways to tally them all. A savant they call me now.

In class, radiators are banging like a calliope on the ocean bottom. I'm third up today. In the hole, as they say—parlance of baseball. Show-and-tell in the civics class of Miss Fontaine. Our lesson: *Share the story of one of the world's religions, not necessarily your own.*

Half the class went up to speak this week, and the rest will do so after the holiday. But not one in tongues till me. Most brought the Good Book and read some familiar passage. Read like they were robots and believed not a single golden word. Two new Arabian students who came over with their families for the horse country showed how they find Mecca to pray toward every day. Miss Fontaine tried to tell them despite what their compass said they'd been point-ing themselves in the wrong direction all year.

A few in class said not much of anything. Can't they find them-selves a faith to believe in? Those giant pinwheels of stars they spy every time that Hubble peeks out into the vast night? Or all the little sprites out in nature? Primitive man used to know them, and so did I when I was young. Saw those imps out in the darkest woods. Till I found the true path. Then they were gone to me.

Suzie's twitching in the tool chest now. Sssshhhh, Suzie. She can sense my worry, and I can feel hers. She knows she's—on deck.

"My name is Darby Ruth Funellion. Some of you know me. All o' you seen me. Sorry I smile so. Can't help it. First, let me just say I thank y'all for this schooling you have blessed me with. I love my school uniform, I do, so I will not sully it now with any damnable secretions. Sometimes when I testify it can get a mess on."

I take off my maroon tunic and tartan skirt, standing there in Granny's petticoat of an older fashion, with her ole girdle peek-a-booing through beneath. To me these are comfortable hand-me-downs, no reason not to get more use from them. I hear the kids all titter-whisper. I do not look direct. I never look direct. They begin their rain of catcalling. My dental flaws, the redness of my hair. Miss Fontaine tries her best to shush them back in line. Such belittlement I do not understand. But it must have a satisfaction to make it so relentless.

"You all got some fine believins, and it's not for me to say mine is any better'n yours, just one more path to righteousness. I—and by I, I mean we—my kin down in Frankton Hollow—well, we believe in deed not speech when it comes to faith."

I shout out of nowhere: "The Spirit! Mark 16! Holy Ghost! Prove it every day! Prove it again and ye walk without sin!"

I need the rhythms now.

"Help me, please, Bobby, with my music," I ask of a quiet student in the first row, who plugs things in for me. I push the sticky button on the beatbox.

"We really rip it up for the Lord down in Frankton. This here is the Signs to Follow Band."

Uncle Carson's bass wells up into a walking throb, buzzing the tiny speakers. Then Tall Paul-Henry's lonely guitar twang shivers out across the room and up my spine. Everyone laughs at my taste in song, but all go silent quick as Suzie comes on out, wriggling and shaking her baby rattle.

"This here is an eastern diamondback, most deadly of the deadly, and we got thirty dozen. Not so many in the winters. My Uncle Travis swapped a mess of copperheads for her and her brother. She's a baby, Suzie is. She don't know herself enough not to bite. The young ones bite at shadows. Can't hold their poison in. If my faith should falter, if I even let one drop of that old doubt seep in—I will die in front of you today. Mark 16:18! *They shall take up serpents; and if they drink any deadly thing, it shall not hurt them . . . they shall recover. . . . Behold, I give unto you power to tread on serpents and scorpions, and over all the power of the enemy: and nothing shall by any means hurt you. . . .* Luke 10:19! I will now manifest whole and put to mortal test my faith everlasting, or I will meet the Lord—a failed believer. And he will slap me down a fiery hellhole to lay with that hairy red Devil for eternity."

Class has hushed up but good, and Miss Fontaine stammers, but no words leave her lips. She seems to have the grip. I pull out a small rusty can. As I thumb the cap off, a foulness invades the room with an oily garage smell—cuts your lungs acoughin'. I squeeze the green-yellow from it into a thick goblet of old cobalt glass.

"This here is turpentine, and I will drink of this demon blood. I do believe, and it can do me no harm. It may blindeth the eye for a spell and stingeth the lips, but I believe, so it will not harm. It will pass on through me like the nail in his flesh. Pain is the glue of God. Glue of God, hold thine to me."

I drink the turpentine. The glass cracks in my hand. I hold my wound up to show the bloody hole in my palm. Both palms now, though I was cut in only one. Something vomits up inside, but I choke it all back down and lick the bubbling foam from the curl of my lips. Smiling all the while, free of thought. Lips moving now, something ancient taking hold. My eyes roll white back up in my skull. Some dusty ole archangel comes hurtling down from the heavenly rafters to channel through me, washing splendor through my every cell. I will be his mortal vessel for a spell. My voice drops down two of those octaves and growls out, "There were serpents in my cradle. I was born a special one, and I lay in grace."

I slide the lid off the other box I brought and place my hands inside. Three scorpions scuttle up my arms, making my hairs and skin all goosey. More kids in class are squirming now, a couple running for the doors. But the rest cannot look away. Told you so, told you so. They will hold witness to the power of my faith. Words welling up now. I twitch and shuffle with the beat moving me toward rapture.

*"Now I lay me down to die*
*To be reborn . . .*
*By dawn sunrise*
*Devil may tempt*
*Devil will trick*
*But he come near*
*I make that devil sick*
*He come again*
*Right back quick*
*I beat that devil*
*With my Jesus Stick."*

For a moment, Suzie goes stiff as wood, and I whirl her over my head like the staff of Moses. Those cruel beauties and even a boy or two are crying now. On the norm I would just do a little shakin', a little glossolalia, but this ole angel, he wants a big ruckus like that night at the tent show in Effington. A greater *proving*. Sometimes unbelievers need an Audie Murphy—a ride to hell and back. The angel asks in a voice inside me, *Darby Ruth, are you willing today, though it take a toll on thee, and you'll need you three weeks sleep to shake it off?*

*Yes, please. Slap the smiles from these silly children,* I answer him.

Here we go. Suzie wants never to harm me, but I squeeze her fangs against her will into my fingertip just a pinch. She slumps to sleep, and that finger gnarls up, leaking yellow pus. Gangrene grows just like that from my hand, up the veins like black crystals of a rotting frost. Across to my heart, beating so hard it shakes the windows now. Racing faster—faster—then a sudden stop.

Sheer black of midnight spews from my maw and keeps spilling till the room is dark as obsidian floating in ink at the bottom of a mile-deep well. Class half frozen in time. We are nowhere now. In the shadow of the sun. Sermons roar from my lips in the ecstasy of Aramaic. Then, slowly, golden light grows up all around. Faces slowly look at one another, unable to move the rest of themselves. I stare into their eyes now. For the first time

Oh, how these beauties can burn with their words—*dog meat*—*virgin freakling!* They brag of boys inside them, fumbling and quickly spent. And that's so special? Compared to this? My every corpuscle filling now with an eternal, all-knowing divine behemoth, blazing with loins of heavenly fire! Filling me up—filling me whole! And He don't fumble, and He's never spent.

The bellow of Jehovah rattles from my lips, and everyone's flesh begins to melt away, dripping into pools of skin and guts on the floor. Save for their natural-born eyes, left floating in the sockets of their skulls, we are rendered down to skeletons. At first all seem to be the same. One no different than the next. At last—all of us on even par. Then one notices a few are blessed with better rib cages, more perfect hip bones. Here we go again. Always something left to divide one against another. Until we are all dust again, I fear.

"Now look, it is written, stitched on bone: your fate and your damnation!"

The skeletons look at fancy scribbling on their femurs and what have you—royal blue words tattooed on the alabaster.

"You, Colleen Boudreaux, will die from drinking on July 6, 2032! Your lifeline is two degrees from where it should be. Two hundred fifteen of your prayers were not sincere. You, Otto Swain, on some future day shall be an adulterer! Seven times in deed, and two thousand seven in the heart. You, Millard Judkins, will become a cheater of your business partner! You will steal eighty thousand, nine hundred fifty-two dollars and keep it in your daddy's coal bin. This is who you are today. A fraction of your future-tallied sins. Only you can wash these bones clean. Jesus Only and Signs to Follow! Holy Ghost in Frankton Hollow!"

A whirlpool of bright blood swirls from the floor, rising impossible fast till the room is consumed by a red so bright and pure you can't remember any other color. The thunder of a house-size heartbeat starts up. Tenfold in power. A hundred. A thousand. Bones are gone. Flesh gone in the next great thumping—until we are only floating pairs of eyes, alone inside *His* beating heart. We rush up from *His* aorta, through *His* veins, up into *His* eyes. Our eyes in *His* eyes. Looking down from the cross at Golgotha. Lightning strikes. A giant Jesus tear squeezes out past us—washing us in *His* eternal love.

Lightning strikes again, and all flashes into whiteness now. Endless and forever. A storm of angel wings fluttering, caressing—restoring human flesh back to everyone. Better than before. Exalted. Perfect. Pimples gone. A cleft palate healed. Someone's wine-stain birthmark fading fast. All but me. *Why, Lord, why not me? Your best believer, why am I left this way? I know you must have your reasons.*

I have become a coiled serpent. What the angel lets them see now. Sisterhood with Suzie—of cold blood and scales, of flicking forked tongues. I grow inside the whiteness of this giant shell. Up from curly worm into full-born, ready for bursting. One tooth, long and shining. The eggtooth. Its only purpose to bite a way out from within egg walls at birth. I begin to nibble, to leave this orb for the next. I grow, stretching up to bite a hole, revealing the infinite stars beyond.

I am holding Suzie, standing again in front of class. Back to natural wonder. In an eye blink the spell has broken. Bells are ringing. My quarter hour passed in but a moment. The class watches as the tiniest of snakeheads bites her way clear of the fragile sac with her single minuscule fang. The room coos with nervous awe. I say nothing more. I have gone beyond words again.

The class mumbles as I sit. There's some light applause, like maybe how it was for Lincoln back there at Gettysburg. They know they have witnessed something monumental and that they will, none of them, ever be the same.

Far as performance goes, I think it was at least a triple. The ole angel says an inside-the-park home run. Parlance of baseball. Then he is gone.

I take Susie out back and let her weave away through the thick bluegrass. I smile. But I am always smiling.

# HER GREAT BLUE

In April, on the island of Terzoza, the morning breeze stalls, and local skuas resting on the wind expend an extra avian calorie to flap themselves aloft again, dipping past the first *ecoturistas* of the season arriving on the beach at Sambrina Bay. The black sands are as promised in the cruise line's brochure. The birds scan for morsels amidst the alabaster thighs and doughy arms of an aging group who hail from Hamburg. What strange manatees they seem from on high.

A dozen women lay out a meal to share—*Schweinshaxe, Grünkohl,* and ample chunks of marzipan. A tiny girl in a yellow dress yawns her candy-sour breath and dashes down to the lapping waves and back. Besides their guide, Rolf, there is only one other man, a Greek, perhaps, who joined the excursion late and seems out of place among them.

The sparsely peopled rock of Terzoza is an orphan strewn far from sibling isles along the mid-Atlantic rift—the great wound of the Earth where Pangaea was torn asunder. An extra day trip by shuttlecraft from the main vessel, this particular lagoon is well worth the jaunt during the proxigean spring tide. *A supreme vantage from which to behold the rutting of randy whales. Hookup central for all spry cetaceans in the Atlantic!* boasts a new publicity spiel, trying to cater to a younger demographic, though the median age of today's visitors appears to be just this side of mild stroke.

The first whale of the morning, a young humpback, uproots from the skin of the sea, undulating aloft—hang time the equal of any Jordon leapage. It thunders back down with a thousand-gallon halo splash. The sound reaches shore a few seconds after the sight as the *frauen* scurry to aim lenses in the same vicinity in the hope of more wonderment.

The Germans, who have been told these waters are too rough for a boating view, notice the *canoa*, an old whaling vessel, rocking on the swells out near the twin haystack rocks. Only one person can be seen aboard the dilapidated craft, which would hold half a dozen on a whaling run, and from the sun bloom of long hair, the figure seems likely female.

"A stunning one," remarks a *frau* focusing her 200mm Zeiss. The Greek grabs her camera without permission, and as he sights the woman out upon the waves, a sliver of smile graces his knife-scarred face.

Muriel Woods, alone on the vessel, yanks the rubber of her wet suit flush and zips it sealed. She is still a world-class beauty in her nebulous forties, her sun-taxed skin Pollacked with delicate freckling—hallmark of a brief It-Girl look she'd enjoyed (*Vogue Paris* and *Numéro* covers). Once glorious auburn locks have dreaded into an array of gorgon tendrils from lack of a proper brush, living on harsh Terzoza all winter, and been burnished by the elements back to their true ruddy hue.

A massive *Balaenoptera musculus* begins to climb verticular and time—slows—down. Muriel awe-freezes as the great blue whale rises so close she can gaze deep into a magnificent eye at the apogee of the thrust, all the way back to golden filigree in a retina reflecting the low sun. She could almost stretch her fingers out to touch the metropolis of encrustment clinging to its elephantine skin. Muriel feels an intimacy both fearsome and sublime, as if this vast creature has peered into some dormant chamber of her soul as the rorqual slides back, exploding brine across the boat. The single biggest creature she has ever seen. The largest the world has too.

A vivid childhood memory wells up—three ill bowheads contorted on the sands at Cannon Beach when Muriel was twelve. Her father, Gus, trying to ease her horror.

*Whales never really get a chance to sleep, Murie. And they must remember to inhale and exhale each time—for all their lives. But if they can steer clear of a whole world trying to kill 'em, a few live on for centuries. Oldest animals on earth. These beasts have surely had a splendid life.*

She remembers the warmth of his callused hand against her neck as both stepped closer through the spray of the crashing surf. Gus taught Muriel to always stare calamity right in the face—never look away. They joined others on the beach trying to usher the bowheads back out to sea, but the tide was against them, and there was no will left in their hearts.

*When whales get too sick, some want to return to land and take their last breaths there. Has to make you wonder—do they remember living beyond the ocean, millions of years ago, when fins were legs? Distant relative of the hippo, they say. Herds of them roamed and shook the earth. They've just come home, Pumpkin.*

All three whales had perished. One carcass became famous for a freak explosion while being hauled through a coastal town—splattering storefronts with fetid blubber, leaving a stench that took years to subside.

Her father had been close to sixty when Muriel was born. Of a lust mistake, nothing close to love. A psoriatic ex-catcher building sets for *The Tempest* at the Ashland Shakespeare Festival who'd spent

40

a drunken night with an Irish understudy. The next season, the lass returned for a week, left the tiny Muriel, then miraged again.

Gus did his damnedest to sober up and provide, homeschooling Muriel in back road motels while scouting the bush leagues for the Giants' organization in a boat of an old woody Chrysler. He'd owned it since it was new, kept it primo within and without. Always had a dog-eared WPA guide handy for each state they drove through, from which he spouted lore and knowledge. *Pickle Capital of the World. Birthplace of the guy who invented the Slinky. The exact spot where the Paiute, Wovoka, first performed the Ghost Dance.* He taught her how to tear an engine down, cast a fly, make gunpowder from scratch and umpteen other things.

Gus lived on till he was seventy-five, the year Muriel began to blossom from a gangly, toothy thing into her singular natural beauty. He knew he'd done his best to prepare her, that she would have some measure of fulfillment out in the world and he could let his bones expire. He was, if not conscious of every breath he'd taken, grateful still for each day he'd been blessed with Muriel.

Down Mexico way, after assessing a southpaw from San Felipe, he'd left her with the nuns and paddled out into the midnight waters of the Sea of Cortez, heading for a pod of whales venting in the moonlight. Never to return. Muriel has always dreamt her father is out there somewhere still, swimming among them.

A chorus of welcome carries on the wind, and Muriel looks shoreward to the Germans calling out to her. She waves back and starts to smile, then quickly covers her mouth, though from the distance they could hardly see the damage: black gaps of two lower teeth missing, startling flaws to her extraordinary features. Worse, revealed at full grin, four upper incisors chipped jack-o-lantern jagged; the lamprey mouth of a Siren, courtesy of a hard fall on icy steps last January. If and when she has the means to escape this place and make it to a modern town, she thinks she might choose to leave a few snags unfixed—for character.

Muriel should be frightened lolling out here among behemoths fucking, but of more concern right now is that her longtime sugar daddy, Jimmy Adelaide, has gone below again this morning, forgetting to fully refill his tank. There should be no more than twenty minutes of oxygen left, and the powerful tide will shift in less than thirty. He's lost all track of time, delirious to have found an ancient shipwreck caught at the bottom of the outcrop rocks. They should be gunning the Evinrude, hightailing it back to the village to try again *amanhã*. Muriel must go fetch him, and that is the last thing she wishes to do, having nearly perished from the bends on a dive in Fiji years ago. She throws a coiled rope, and with an expert clove hitch secures the *canoa* to a protuberance on the rocks, then checks the air in the backup tank. Their diving gear is decades old, hardly adequate for even a simple dive, let alone a perilous one. Her hands begin to twitch; she closes her eyes, inhaling deeply to still the tremors.

Her immense new friend eases up gracefully, barely rippling the surface—seeking only another look at her.

🕊

Last August, after they'd caught *The Book of Mormon* matinee, Muriel was chiding Jimmy as he flashed his new watch in the back of Aquagrill.

"But will it keep time any better than a Swatch?"

He blushed as she clucked her tongue and rolled her huge, celadon eyes. Nevertheless, he spent four minutes explaining precisely how the mechanism of the Patek Philippe Calatrava puts a lesser timepiece to shame.

At Tourneau, Jimmy had coveted a higher echelon with still more complication, the *Nautilus Rose* or the *World Time*, but hesitated, the great fortune he managed having recently plummeted on a severe downtick. Jimmy'd always had the golden touch and was sure it was just an ebb, a transient thing—thought it bad luck to have hedged on the choice.

His driver appeared at the rear door of Aquagrill, and nods were exchanged. He was late for something urgent. He pecked Muriel's cheek, then signed the Amex slip without gratuity—holding the moment, content her perfect smile was among his many possessions—then removed the Patek Philippe and laid it on the waiter's server book, zeroing out the young man's student loans. Jimmy knew the gesture made Muriel giddier than any couture he could surprise her with at Fashion Week; she would always be more pleased cajoling out of him six-figure donations to *Médecins Sans Frontières* than taking his planned decadent getaways to Mustique or the Maldives.

Ease of companionship with older men came naturally for Muriel. Professors in New York, mentors and photographers in Paris and Milan were invariably these; she counted very few lovers of her own generation. It was an easy pop-shrink for others to factor in her father's age, the loss of him early, but she *didn't give a hoot*, as Gus would say. The pleasures of a seasoned gentleman always trumped the intoxicating chaos of young testosterone for her. It was nothing to boast of, but she enjoyed being held upon a pedestal, preferring to be *adored*, as older mates would gladly do.

They'd only recently gone public, at least in NYC, after eleven years of her being *kept*, and it had been just weeks since Jimmy's wife, Kaye, had lost her long battle with Parkinson's. He loved them each, in much different ways, and though it was déclassé to couple up so soon, there were no children involved and not much family near, so they made a bald display of it. *Let tongues wag—we're out of the shadows now.*

🐦

Muriel looks toward shore a last time, hearing Teutonic ooohing drift on the wind as a right whale corkscrews a belly flop back into the surf, then pulls her mask on, securing the mouthpiece, and slides otterlike over the side.

Instantly she is enveloped in another universe—a panorama thick with swirling life. Pure splendor, deeply blue and endless. A manta ray furls itself just below her feet—a magic carpet she could ride if she wished. Dolphins herd a cyclone of mackerel toward the surface, then sky invades the sea as a flock of shearwaters propels itself thirty feet below, using wings as fins to dive and snatch prey.

Muriel looks down the length of Jimmy's rope, which disappears from sight ten fathoms below, and begins pulling herself hand over hand toward the faint wedge at the base of the two basalt columns. Her heart hard-squeezes in her chest as a hammerhead sidles up, impossibly spaced obsidian eyes belying nothing, before drifting on with a mere flick of tail.

She hangs a moment, remembering Fiji. Forced to surface when her tank malfunctioned, she'd risen eighty feet on one last dying breath. Nitrogen in her tissue bubbled and spasmed her with infinite pain—elbows and knees unhinging from their sockets. Three days in the hyperbaric. She was lucky to walk again, but the healing sent her back on opiates after ten years clean. She's sworn never to dive, no matter what, but he needs her—Jimmy needs her.

Something eclipses the light filtering below—a hand of Zeus waving over Poseidon's lair. Muriel turns back toward the surface to see the mass of the ancient blue whale passing between her and the *canoa*. Same one she had her moment with, she's sure—covered with a colony of things across its ribbed underside. Silhouettes of other Mysticeti can be seen all around, ballooning their ventral pouches to vacuum up krill by the ton, but this beast seems to have little appetite this morning—only fascination with a ginger-haired sylph.

The blue whale's flipper gently grazes the rope, plucking it taut a moment, then lets it rip through the water in a blur of vibration. Muriel senses the thrum as the cord settles back into place, still intact. *Moby Dick on bass*. She tries not to laugh and ruin the cadence of her breathing as she pulls herself farther on, toward bubbles rising from what's left of an ancient ship resting on the bottom. The blue whale drifts down, not far behind her.

*Bubbles are good. Bubbles mean life—Jimmy still breathing.* Muriel squints at a pinpoint of intense blue flickering on the side of the hull, recognizing the underwater cutting torch lying there. Jimmy had taken it below to open Davy Jones' Locker, but there is no Jimmy in sight.

As she descends the final league, the reef truly comes to life, churning with wriggling and undulating biota at every turn. The liquid murmuration of the schools shifting on collective whim; crustaceans happy to be exactly what they are, scuttling their ragged claws across a noisy sea floor.

Her flashlight leads her toward the murk within a ten-foot hole in the calcified galleon that has become a reef itself over the centuries. Inside, the rope disappears into a clusterfuck of rotten nets and fishing line, fouled too with plastic—six-pack rings and remnants of preformed packaging, the ghostly dregs of convenience. Muriel sweeps the light and finds Jimmy caught up in the Gordian mass, weakened by the struggle, but more so from a gash down his forearm, which pours his crimson out.

Muriel grabs the strap of his tank and kicks fins hard as she can. Both rise from the hole, but the huge fibrous clot follows, and as their upward thrust abruptly ceases, the dead tentacles lasso around her gear, ensnaring her as well. Jimmy's face is bluing, limbs in early-stage paroxysm. His eyelids lift, but panic is not beneath. He seems gripped by a powerful tranquility, as if gazing upon an angel. A plume rises from his wound into a nimbus pinking in the faint light. Muriel tries not to show alarm, reaching through the clinging webbing to shut off his nearly expired tank. She begins to share her mouthpiece, letting Jimmy nurse her air awhile. Like a babe lulled by a comforting teat, he is reluctant to give up the gift when she needs it back for her next breath. *Jimmy—a name for a boy, not a man of sixty-seven. What tore your flesh? An antique nail, an eel?* As a thresher swoops past, Muriel rethinks her efforts to free them. *Perhaps there is sanctuary here. Camouflage is the first rule of the sea.*

Two lovers float, bound and twisting in a blood cloud with devils circling down.

🕊

In late September, Jimmy had looked out on his imperial view of Madison Avenue and told Muriel she could pick any place on his vintage globe and he would take her there. In five-star comfort, of course. He'd promised a Grand Tour, hinting of permanently embracing expatriate life.

She considered the possibilities contained on the surface of the Weber Costello, a '60s orb perched atop a polished silver airplane, with its oceans black and countries all wrong in Africa and the old Iron Curtain. Muriel spun it through a dozen days, then stepped away and fished out her masticated gum. It was a little game they'd played before. She coiled herself in a windup Gus had taught her and threw a strike at the dusky blur. The wad made a soft splat and hung there.

"Lapland! Patagonia! Ulan Bator!" she chanted as if it were roulette, willing a number to come up. Between swimsuit shoots at exotic locales, Jimmy's luxe vacations, and her father's love of geography, Muriel knew her Earth, every inch of it.

"Rapa Nui! The Kalahari! Fez!"

As the globe wheeled to a stop, Jimmy laughed and ran to show her the islands that were closest to where her Dentine stuck—a green monster on a dark sea. Muriel noticed he'd slid the gum many inches west from where it had actually landed, not bothering to clean away the snail trail. This was all gesture, not any real choice. Jimmy knew exactly where he was headed.

In October, they'd flown a charter to the capital on the eastern end of the archipelago. The last thing he charged before Amex froze the account. The stupendous gains made had unraveled via some complex formula he'd devised. Schadenfreude would soon be ricocheting around the financial sector about Jimmy—the autodidact quant with the magic returns, biting the dust as bad as Corzine. *Live by the algorithm, die by the algorithm.* Their scheduled destination was Marseille, and the islands were a stopover, but the couple never returned to the plane from lunch, absconding with just a portion of their luggage. Jimmy had initially passed it off to Muriel as a whim— *Let's be spontaneous for once. Damn the itinerary.*

Down at the wharf, he hired a fisherman named Lopo to take them west to far Terzoza. A squat, sea-leathered man, he'd jerry-rigged a rusting outboard to an old rowing vessel once used for whaling. It choked to death three times on the long trip over.

It was there, engineless in open waters, where Jimmy had tried to broach a version of the truth, whispering and sobbing to Muriel as Lopo smacked the motor with a monkey wrench. Mercurial markets, jealous sabotage; it didn't matter how—it was gone, all gone.

"Stay till spring. That's all I ask."

Besides lavishing her with years of extravagant perks, Jimmy had also been there for her through a brutal spinal surgery and a long, contorted drug rehab. *The man had just lost both wife and fortune; his mistress ditching would have to wait.*

"As long you need, Jimmy."

At least her words kept him in the boat; he'd been that far at the end of his rope. This would be an opportunity, Muriel thought, to discover what stuff her core was still made of. It had been a while since her mettle had been tested.

What wasn't broached: people would be looking for Jimmy. People who meant to do him harm and knew how to do it well. A major investor in his fund—an Albanian arms merchant, Leotrim Zughli—was his greatest worry. If Jimmy could not repay this man's principal, his life would be worth less than the sixteen hundred dollars left in his pocket.

◆

Muriel checks both tanks again, scanning above and behind for predators. At first her view holds none, but as snouts triangulate the beacon of Jimmy's blood, killers begin stacking up like jets over JFK.

The largest of the great whites slaloms her way. Muriel hangs limp, trying to impersonate kelp. She feels the encompassing shadow moving swiftly above again, and the blue whale dives to thwart the attack, ramming the shark headlong like a bumper car, bruising cartilage, then smacking a flipper—sending it tumbling away.

Muriel is astonished by what her mega fauna friend has done on her behalf, as it pirouettes some marine equivalent of a touchdown dance. She is transfixed as the eye of him passes near, blinking slowly, then glides on.

She turns to snake a hand through the tangle, petting Jimmy's brow. His eyes remain tight-lidded. She knows him all too well; Jimmy has seen the shark fest—it's that he *won't* look, not can't. She switches him onto his own air and takes hers back, then attempts again to raise them, but their problem is greater than rope. Weight. Within a canvas bag around his belly, she sees the glint of untarnished coins— *gold*. Muriel reaches for the bag, and Jimmy's hands swallow like an anemone, bending her fingers back, eyes staring primal. He shrinks back into the mass of netting. She tussles with him, trying to get him to face her, but he resists, oblivious to the dire situation. Their motion mimics struggling prey, and barracuda flash over.

One bites her ankle in a furious instant, tearing through her Achilles.

🐦

Lopo had managed to ferry Muriel and Jimmy on through the rough autumn seas. On Teroza, the blood native to the rest of the archipelago was also mixed that of Berber pirates, Basque mutineers from the Portuguese fleet, along with Sephardim diaspora'd only halfway to the New World—an inbred line of a few extended outcast families, who until the recent ecotourist boom had seldom welcomed anyone from elsewhere in their midst.

Jimmy bought Lopo considerable lamb and port at the only inn on Terzoza, pleased to learn no more vessels would arrive till spring. The shipwrecks were all on other islands was Lopo's initial claim, but later he was lubricated enough to recall finding a gold coin during a freak-ish low tide when he was a child—out by the twin rocks of Sambrina Bay. Thought it was a candy wrapped in foil and broke a tooth on it. Jimmy could barely contain himself, even as the fisherman warned: *Those waters—treacherous. Only at the peak hour of a strong tide can you even dream of diving there.*

The establishment they dined in was formerly a wooden slaughter-house from the whaling era, and Muriel shivered as Lopo told tales of it being filled knee-deep with viscous blubber, slick with spermaceti, told of the relentless search for the shit-pearl of ambergris. Of a four-hundred-pound heart hung on hooks, smoked for the village feast.

Lopo had tried to assuage her with the claim Terzozans had ceased their killing over three decades before the other islands. And volun-tarily. The creatures they worshipped long ago had communicated with them and forged a truce, or so legend held. Still, she felt atroc-ity permeating the space, no matter the many candles that burned.

Muriel remembered how Gus had been incensed that of all the men on the earth one might welcome into Camelot, Jackie Kennedy had chosen Onassis. He'd rant how the millionaire shipping magnate became a billionaire from his wanton illegal hunting during the world ban—driving the endangered blue and others to near extinction.

Muriel had once broached her theorem to a Kennedy cousin who pestered her for a date: It wasn't weather, nor the hubris of flying blind on instruments without sufficient hours. Not even the family curse. Whales had jammed the controls somehow with their powerful sonic abilities. It was payback.

Muriel refused to lodge at the inn, so Lopo arranged for them to tend the island's iconic structure, the *Ciclope* for the winter. A temple of sorts, built upon a cliff above the village.

A shallow lagoon with twin outcrops was the rumored locus where the Spanish carrack, *The Mazenita*, had gone down in 1585, ripped up by the rocks while hiding from profiteers. The lone survivor of the wreck had stated such in a rare vellum account of the tragedy that Jimmy had procured at great expense years ago. It was a secret dream to someday go searching for it. Now it was a necessity. Jimmy kept a relentless eye on the rocks all winter, waiting for the tranquil waters of spring, making sure no one would beat him to the punch. The ship's fortune in gold could repay the greater portion of the losses; at least make amends with those who would end him. It was his last hope.

❧

Muriel and Jimmy sink slowly back toward the hole in the vessel, still engulfed in the infernal netting. Spotting the underwater torch just below, strobing against the hull like a dying sparkler, she reaches through the twine to grab the handle, looking away from the blinding tip, and uses it to burn through ropes and lines.

She is still caught in the detritus when a mako fins up from the ocean floor, and Muriel cranks the torch and roasts a wound through its gills. The shark flails off spilling a cloud of its own juices. *Tell the others, bitch. Eat someone else today!* She looks around for her protector, wondering if he's gone fickle as all males do in time. No, there he is—drifting cockeyed just above, seeming in awe of what she's done.

Muriel checks her wound—blanched rosy-white, but a darkness flowing from a star-shaped fissure. She bites down on her mouthpiece—so hard a fragile chunk of front tooth snaps off and slips past her lips, gleaming in the water. She reaches to retrieve it, but something bright and yellow swoops in and swallows it first.

She lifts a bended knee, reaching back to pass blue flame across her flesh. *Agony and blinding light.* Her tendon cringes into a blackened mass. The letting, though, is staunched.

As Muriel passes out, she senses the great cetacean easing down, watching over, savoring the redolence of her veins.

❧

Midwinter, Muriel had awoken in the drafty hollow of the *Ciclope* and rustled a stick to get the embers breathing again. She looked around the spartan interior—bales of hay they slept on, cracks in the wall absurdly stuffed with Valentino and Chanel. She recalled donkeys laden with Louis Vuitton winding up the serpentine steps to the cliff high above the village. The edifice had been built in ancient times: an elongated structure made from strange mother-of-pearl adobe that glimmered with a spectral cast—remnants of lost Atlantis, some Terzozans believed. No windows but for narrow open slits that funneled wind with a harmonic drone. From this vantage could be seen Sambrina Bay below, and beyond, the distant cinder cone of the nearest island.

Muriel had set a tin of thick goat stew on the coals and closed her eyes, imagining the wind to be a four-hundred-horsepower purr, remembering Gus cooking TV dinners on the engine block of the Pontiac. Her dad had devised a whole system—a drive of fifty miles at seventy mph for frozen meals. In harsh times it might have been roadkill rabbit, if fresh enough, broiling on that V8. *A sin to let good meat go to waste. There's kids starving over there in Catch-as-catch-canistan. Eat up, Pumpkin!*

She watched Jimmy murmuring the Lebanese dialect of his extended family. They were Druze who'd migrated five generations back, building a florist empire in Melbourne and dissolving secular over the years. "You know in Oz, when your career goes down the drain, it spins the other way," he'd joke and perhaps toss a *crikey* here and there, but otherwise there were few remnants of either heritage. Jabril Al-Najjar, chess prodigy and high-school dropout, arrived stateside in the '70s, rebranding himself quite believably as Jimmy Adelaide III, eccentric Delaware *old money*. At least enough to marry into it with Kaye. Chameleon came easy to him. The long winter on Terzoza not so much. He withdrew often into a fetal ball, sleeping sixteen hours a day.

Muriel's tongue felt the wreckage of her teeth; her fingers assessed a swollen face finally shrinking back to normal. Two weeks prior she'd tumbled down a dozen snow-slick steps on the long trek to the village; her mouth smashed again and again until the path made a hairpin turn and feet found purchase to stop the slide. She'd sprawled unconscious for an hour, the goats lapping at the warm spring of her blood.

Now Muriel flickers back to clarity. Jimmy hugs his stash in ropes. Sharks nip each other, crazed by hemoglobin. The crusty rorqual glides above like the Goodyear Blimp. She checks her cauterized wound. Nothing oozing from it now, but the brine stings deep.

Muriel burns through more strands of rope and plastic, but there seems to always be another holding somewhere. She hasn't prayed in twenty years, but she'll try now—to the Trinity the nuns failed to imprint upon her soul, to her father's Bahá'í faith, to Neptune and Poseidon, to the unknowable mysteries of the *Ciclope*. Most of all to cetaceans—her chivalrous knights. *Just let me reach the surface without the bends.... I'll never ask for anything again.*

Only minutes left on Jimmy's tank, and he's still enmeshed as Muriel pulls her mortified ankle through the last loop. She is free for the moment, but the infernal tangle threatens to return. She tries one last time to focus Jimmy, but that seems hopeless. The underwater torch will weigh her down, but it will be her Excalibur to wield against sea dragons. She affixes it to her belt, then pulls herself away—up the rope—back toward the *canoa*, air and sky.

After a two-fathom rise Muriel hangs a moment, taking stock of any infusions in her blood, looking down at Jimmy slowly writhing inside the great knot, encircled by predators. *The man never said a cruel word in eleven years. His generosity knew no bounds. And you are leaving him now, in peril.* Muriel heads back, then hesitates.

*Stop Hamleting!*

She cranes her neck to view the faint, wavering light of the distant surface, but before she can make her next indecision, her bones hear something. A rumbling low frequency throttles the world—then, from the opposite end of the audio spectrum, it is skewered by high-pitched cetacean cries. Nausea seizes her, and she watches the blue whale rolling over as if roasted on a spit. Every sea mammal in the same mad distress. This is not any sort of play. The whales are herded by dolphins away from the rocks, away from shore. All but her Great Blue—descending one more time, bringing his eye within inches of her. *Is leviathan in love? Offering her a ride?* Muriel reaches toward the thick ribbing of his belly; her fingers search for some niche but are cut by barnacles as she tries to grab hold. Before she can attempt any sort of mounting, bones ache again from a second rumbling, and the blue is stunned, keeling off as a forest of trapped methane bubbles up from the ocean floor. Algae afire with excitation brighten the view a phosphorescent green. As far as she can see, the sea bottom shudders with movement, kicking up silt and crustaceans.

The ancient hull tumbles over, pulling Jimmy below. In the seconds before the waters cloud opaque, Muriel observes the ocean cease its perfect dance: schools of fish bumping into one another; sharks in abject fear, huddling together for solace. The cessation, for a moment, of the eternal food chain.

She pulls and kicks herself below fast as she can, one-legged. The surface roils; there is nowhere to go above. She can feel the pull of the liquid universe moving away from shore. The blue whale faces the direction of the beach, working his fluke and flippers madly to circle and leave with the flow, but even the foremost living strength on Earth is no match for the upheaval underway. This is not any normal tide, but some monumental, calamitous event. All things are helpless against it.

Muriel is buttressed against the haystack rocks, held fast in a crevice on the shoreward side as a slipstream of sea life whips backward past her. She expects her life to cease at any next moment, but the will of the water weakens suddenly, and light begins to grow. She has the intense sensation that she is rising as the surface shimmers down—hovering closer, closer—then collapses all around her.

Muriel drops ten feet with an explosion of sound to find herself lying on a beach in the world of air. She picks herself up, resting awkwardly on shredded knees. She removes the fogged mask to behold the roaring surf receding off toward a rising club of smoke in the distant east, leaving the bounty of the sea in its wake—ten thousand finned things quivering in the rocky sands, gasping for their brine.

Moments ago, three hundred billion tons of earth cleaved itself from the side of an erupting volcano on the next island, sliding down a trench three miles deep to displace a mountain of water—yanking the Sambrina surf away to cover the debt. Momentarily. The balloon payback will dwarf the leveraged waters one thousand fold upon its return.

Muriel feels ensorceled in a dream; the haystacks tower stories above her now, the *canoa* dangles from a rope at the precipice. She looks out to what's left of the ancient hull. Watches Jimmy extricate himself from the rotted netting tethering him to the ship—a saving grace against the rogue tide. He peels off his wetsuit and slips free, a hirsute creature, naked but for shorts, ambling over to stand in front of her. Holding a single golden coin. Muriel is startled by his energy. When she'd left him he'd seemed an inch from expiration. She's the addled one now, with one thought only: *Was he aware of my abandonment?*

"Earthquake. The sea went out," he pants, checking the clotting wound on his arm.

Muriel tests a baby step, but her tendon will not hold weight.

"Fukushima, Murie! We have to run—hard as we can—as far up that hill..."

She attempts three pathetic bunny hops and falls to the ground. Jimmy exhales and starts back toward the wreckage of the carrack and the large spew of aurum glinting there. He turns back to her, and in that instant she can see it in his eyes: *fight or flight*. There is no

Prince of Denmark moment for Jimmy. His feet take off before he even told them to.

From where she lies, Muriel watches him shuffling up the beach, slipping on eels and jellyfish. *If he looks back, at least I wasn't only flesh to him.* She counts his steps—one-two-three-four-five-six-seven. She wants to call after him, but she cannot as she counts on. Jimmy does not hesitate, and after eleven, the tally of their years together, she turns away, trying to let him and everything they'd ever had fall away. *Could an aging five-foot-seven man even carry her six-one frame? And who the hell is she to judge, when she'd been ready for the same forsaking?*

Jimmy turns back to see Muriel limping out toward the horizon, not even looking his way. He runs on, across the beach toward the *Ciclope* high upon the hill.

*Shock and awe*—slang of war apropos. A swath of horrific grandeur; cacophony of desperate noise. Muriel is still absorbing the dark gift of the ocean disappearing. *How ancient of a thing to be saved by deus ex machina! You cannot slap the Divine after something like this, even if the price of the favor will surely be your death. You must behold the miracle given. This is a lesson—a last enlightenment.* Muriel decides she will not spend her remaining life adrenalized in fear, or worse, hope. She may have only a matter of seconds or a dozen minutes, maybe more, but she would never make it up the hill in time. She will not attempt to outrun the Reaper. She chooses to be only here in the moment, experiencing every sight and smell, making a memory of each sensation to take with her to the other side of whatever will come.

Muriel steps around a huge devil ray plagued by the change of realms. A fried egg rippling in the foam, robbed of locomotion. She gives the stinger wide berth as it rips the air, looking for something to blame. For a moment she considers letting it pierce somewhere, the cold poison numbing through her, inoculating flesh against greater pain to come. But she lopes on. *Feel it all now—feel everything.*

God's fish tank toppled over, spilling its copious creatures, large and small; colors ultra-vibrant without the filtering of water—all squirming, flopping, drowning in air. She must seem to them an alien come to probe, lording over their immobilized forms. The primary thing Muriel has been in life—a human beauty—is meaningless here among them. All are fantastic beings, equal in allure.

When the sea returns, they'll be too weak to work their fins. The stink of them will be their eulogy; spines and skulls left scattered on the hillside, their epitaph. And Muriel will be strewn among them, her bones confused with the rest. She tries not to think of what's in store, but image overloads from Japan are still fresh from years ago. Water invading land, growing blobs of car tops sloshing into bridges, buildings crumpled like wet papier-mâché. Entire blocks gone in seconds with the mad flow. An amorphous, pitiless Godzilla.

Glancing back to shore with the slightest regret, Muriel spies the shape of Jimmy jog-waddling onto the dry sand and hears shouting on the breeze. It sounds like someone screaming—*bitte*.

Jimmy stops to catch his wind and doubled over looks down at the little girl in the yellow dress. Buried to her waist.

"*Treibsand. Sei vorsichtig!*" she pleads.

He hunkers down and begins digging furiously, as a dog would for a bone. Only then does he notice the group from Hamburg across the way, crying in desperation, all held hostage by the sands.

As the earth shook—they'd risen from their blankets and tote chairs. The girl skipped along the foam line, oblivious. The Greek pulled a gun and looked for something to shoot, but there was nothing. A vast sine wave surged through the earth beneath them and the black sands vibrated in the thrall. Everything found new equilibrium as they began sinking down in the liquefaction—prey of a devouring Earth. When the rumbling ceased, the ground returned with harsh embrace, squeezing their breath like a great python.

Jimmy pulls the little one free, carrying her off toward villagers heading to higher ground. On the incline, he can see the ant-line of them, toting what treasures they can up the zigzag steps to *Ciclope*.

The Greek, buried to his shoulders, is frothing loudly in an unknown tongue as Jimmy passes. *An offer of money to take the precious moments to dig him out? Threats if Jimmy should forsake him?* The knife scars across the man's face—a Tirana Smile cut clownlike at the corners of his mouth—only amplify the little girl's panic. A muffled crack is heard, and a tiny wisp of smoke leaks up through the sands from his buried gun. Then two words in the stream of cursing—Leotrim Zughli—shiver Jimmy. Without thinking, he charges over and kicks the Greek hard in the side of his head. Again and again until he's slumping over and the words have stopped. The Hamburg group is fifty feet away, and all are staring now. *What has this naked, hairy man holding our little one just done?*

Jimmy bolts toward the cliff as the girl howls for her family. He must drag her as she resists, falling to her knees, biting and scratching at him.

As they come to the parade of villagers at the seawall, Jimmy puts the girl in the charge of Xianti, a strong-backed matron who'd come to milk the goats at Ciclope.

"Take her higher. Don't let her go."

Xianti seems to have a sure grasp as Jimmy turns back to see the first of the Hamburg women wriggling free on the beach, helping to dig the others out. And beyond—the still missing ocean.

Muriel limps past a seal pup impaled on a shark's rack of teeth. It squirms away with a chunk missing from its flank. The shark cocks its spine, trying to loose the gray mass hanging halfway from a stretched orifice, then with a flood of onerous goo, an infant squirts out, falling inches to the sand. Its mouth gapes. Muriel can see the fresh wound burned through its gills. It is the same mako who charged her earlier— just a mother now, helpless to protect her child. Muriel can see a depth of water left in a bowl-shaped depression farther out. She picks the small slimed thing up, wrapping bubbles of kelp around it, careful to avoid its gnashing baby fangs. The mother watches as Muriel eases it into the pool. The newborn monster takes to it instantly, king of its tiny sea—attacking a wriggling half-dead eel, ripping it to pieces.

*Nature is as cruel as she is beautiful. Mercy's what makes us human, Pumpkin. Grace for grace, deed by deed.* She has them all inside her now, the little wisdoms of her father. If that is all she's left with, it will be enough.

Muriel is startled by an explosion of water eighty feet high out behind the haystack rocks and hears high-pitched moaning. Birds take flight from perches shellacked with Titian hues of excrement as she ventures out that way, letting the ankle support a greater portion of her weight. Agony has plateaued, no longer incapacitating. *Why give it any favor? This wound will not be healing.*

Circling the rocks, she sees the carrack splayed out in final ruin. Doubloons strewn everywhere against the obsidian sands—twinkling constellations of them. Muriel limps past treasure chests spilling their mother lodes and barely wastes a glance.

The low sun across the wet horizon casts the mirage of a city in the distance. Muriel squints at the illusion, but without her proper glasses, the *Fata Morgana* remains an impressionistic blur. Distracted, she bumps into something large and metallic—a wing, half buried in the sand. The remains of a salt-corroded Beechcraft Bonanza, broken on the rocks.

She moves on toward the cries on the wind, shuffling carefully through the minefield of life—mouths and tentacles, stingers and claws. She counts at least a dozen whales stranded all around, but cares for only one—her Great Blue.

Muriel finally sees him down the beach—a mountain humbled on its side, held awkward by a nest of smaller rocks, ribs straining. She limps straight toward the starboard eye.

The sound of the sea remains distant, but a new din begins to drown the gasping of fish. Birds. Hundreds had risen up to circle round when the waters fled, trying to get their brains around the abnormal shift of things. They'd hung in the sky, perplexed. Were they dreaming a meal this vast laid out before them? But there are thousands now—cormorants and pelicans collecting into jagged galaxies with puffins and petrels. Every beak and wing for fifty miles. A hungry darkness wheeling down for a better look at the impossible providence.

A solitary skua lands—tearing a tripe of gills from a sunfish and taking off. Given sanction, another and another land—severing spines, cracking open crabs. The whole mass murder of them falls to earth and begins to devour everything in sight, the sand pocked with layers of tri-dentations.

Muriel limps her gauntlet through their fluttering ecstasy, watching the blur of fowl attacking the prone marine life. Particularly eyes, she notices; a meme passed among the flock that taking sight is a most delicious thing. All seek the viscous treat with the first wounds inflicted.

A mongrel flock has begun to orbit her immobile leviathan, who vents double-barreled blowholes repeatedly to scatter them off. He watches Muriel staggering closer. *Skin shiny with cuttlefish ink; crown of golden kelp; a face shell-white and eyes as green as a moray.* The whale cannot believe this exquisite creature could ever take notice of such a decrepit old beast of the sea. She steps near and grins her broken Siren's smile wide as she can. *What fine baleen this mermaid has.*

Birds begin to attack the whale in force, and Muriel takes position, standing sentry against the marauders who wish to pluck the prize of all he's seen. She fires up the blue hot arc—singeing the wings of two dive-bombing petrels, then turns back, eyes to giant eye, looking deep into him.

"I won't let them."

His iris cringes darker as the sun breaks through. She presses her world-famous mouth against the sturdy cornea and kisses, leaving lip prints on the surface amidst crust of bacteria.

"You and me."

The blue calls back, clicking with sweet piercing echolocation, some incomprehensible song of love.

Muriel's purpose in life, her last few moments of it, will be to stop the blinding of a noble mammalian king by the spawn of dinosaurs. Joan of Arc this or die trying. She dons goggles and fires the flame full on, till it's leaping inches from the tip. They come screeching and twirling toward her as she slashes them out of the sky—one after another. She summons dormant skills: stagecraft fight techniques, Krav Maga, and the art of hitting the ball with the sweet part of the bat. Gus would be proud to see her now. The more she slays, the more dare to test her. They feign and swoop as she swings the torch again and again, arms aching near their limit as the fowl, finally, seem to have learned the lesson.

The blue explodes a geyser, and salt rain scatters the rest away to find easier meals. Muriel has suffered deep pecks, bleeding now through breaches in the rubber skin. In the lull, she leaves the eye to venture back along the gray wall of him. The whale's length seems endless. She peers around the fluke to see the ocean still gone, but massive forces wrestle now far out on the horizon—water crashing into water. In the eastern sky, a huge vulcan thunderhead boils up into the stratosphere.

A blinding light flashes on the far island and before any sound is heard, the wind recoils. The cloud uproots with crimson streaks of lava, crepuscular rays fanning out behind it for a brief heavenly moment. Muriel stands transfixed. The roar of the eruption arrives long after as the cloud expands until the sun is blotted, inking down to a sick yellow disc, then gone.

A purple twilight falls across the horizon, the chill causing wraiths of vapor to rise from the sands. Another terrible sine wave rumbles deep, liquefying the ground again—sea life sinking down, their carrion too. Muriel, lucky to be standing on rocky crags, hurries back along the length of him.

The whale heaves, shifting oil through its porous skull; then, with a straining flipper, manages to twist into a new position. Muriel comes to where the blue has half-rolled upon its side and sees a large mass on the lower abdomen. Like some other creature hanging there. A parasite? A tumor? Then she has the epiphany—of course, the blue must be—she—and as with the mako shark, a birthing is in progress. The view dims quickly as Muriel begins running her hands over the tightened skin, searching for a face on the newborn. She will attempt to doula again, another act of interspecies sisterhood. She yanks hard on the length of it, trying to help the whale calf out into the last light of the world. At the very tip she finds what could be the infant's blowhole, but can find no eyes, no mouth. Poor deformed child. She pulls with all her might, again and again and again, cursing man's ruination of the sea.

The whole of the cetacean mountain shivers, and without warning, a diaphanous cloud of pinkish semen expels everywhere, splattering her wetsuit and hair, knocking her to the ground. The mass mistook for a child is, in fact, his engorged dork—the world's largest penis. Such a rarefied scatological event should demand considerable disgust, but Muriel can barely afford a startled laugh as a thousand streaks begin to be propelled through the sky overhead—all the way over from the new eruption. Everywhere things are pelted with the heated tephra. Gluttonous birds, too full for flight, smashed into the sand. Semimolten rocks pummel down with yelps of steam. Some the size of ping-pong balls, a few as big as microwaves, crater the horizon. Gravity's pumice rainbow. A streaking rock smacks the blue whale's hind, burning into him, sizzling down through layers of blubber. His bulk undulates in agony.

Muriel hurries back to his eye. Trying to blot the rest of the world from her thoughts, she looks into him again. *Hold on. You are a fortress! You are built to withstand the fury.*

The huge jaws unhinge, and a flood of squid and krill spews forth as his tongue uproots the meal onto the sands. A softer tone rumbles forth. An overture. Muriel retreats as pelting hits near—stepping back into the giant maw. Fortress indeed. For the first time, she lets herself have the dizziest hope she could still survive. She climbs farther in and ropes herself to the comb of his baleen so as not to be Jonah'd as his huge tongue gently cuddles her up in the folds at the tip. Muriel will ride the wave here inside these ramparts.

The whale begins a long slow inhalation, storing up every cubic meter of air it can for what is coming. Muriel looks out from inside the crescent of his smile as the mouth slowly closes—molten rocks streaking across the horizon. Just before the view inks out, she hears her name being screamed on the wind. Then all is darkness.

Jimmy shouted *Muriel* three more times, walking lost through the fog. Light of primordial war pulsing all around him. The nearby haystacks were hit with volcanic ammo, and he found bearings, heading out through the broken woodstone of the carrack to the everlasting gleam of fortune held in its belly all these years. The ocean was still obscured, but the sound of its fearsome charge could be heard growing to crescendo, racing toward the beach.

The voice of the Greek called out behind him. "All this belong to Leotrim now—not scumsbag."

Jimmy did not turn around. He stepped farther into the vast cache of golden things, dropping to his knees. A man who'd lost everything, made whole again. He watched an emerald-crusted goblet inhabited by a hermit crab scuttle near him, and he laughed.

*At this moment it is mine.*

He never heard the gunshot. The roar of the cresting wave drowned out every decibel. His face fell to the coins and nuggets, and he wished he could breathe them in. That his skin was painted with their luster; that a molten form of it was pumping in his veins through a gilded heart.

Jimmy tried not to think of them—Kaye and Muriel, the loves of his life. Gold was all he could bear. He lifted his head one last time, just before the crack of the second shot, and looked east. There was a brief clearing in the fog ahead of pressure from the wave. It could be seen climbing skyward, impossibly high—a living Everest capped with snow of a boiling surf. Jimmy glimpsed, for an instant, acres of magnificent architecture lying below its path across the ocean floor—minarets and columns, pyramids and domes and so much more; shapes and wonders never seen before, never even imagined. An antediluvian city resting there, half buried from an ancient lava flow.

The wave obliterated the last memory of it—for all time.

Muriel had faced death as she'd been birthed—in darkness and brine—as the blue whale was swept off violently between the haystack rocks. Not only were these Scylla and Charybdis for him, but all possible fates seemed perilous. Barnacles were scraped from skin, skin from blubber, meat from bones. An undertow of immense proportions tumbled the rorqual down, dragging him along the ocean floor, holding his blowhole far below. Starved of air, he weakened quickly as all things charged landward in a vast determined force. The whale channeled air from his lungs up into the mouth chamber for his mermaid to breathe. Finally, a rising ebb within the maelstrom caught the whale, lifting him surface-ward, to bob above the foam again. He breathed deep and worked his fluke and flippers to right himself, taking steps, *running* toward land.

The sea rose steadily up the incline of arrogant Terzoza, which dared to stand in its way. It climbed the cobblestone stairs in seconds and swept away the exhausted Hamburg group, who had nearly made it to the summit. The mad tide lifted up toward *Ciclope*, and with one last sigh, strained over the lip of land, crashing millions of gallons into a dry crater beyond, filling it to the brim.

The volcanic rage sated, the sea slunk back to the dark sands from whence it came, calming to a normal fury. The great blue whale was left resting on a precipice where it could view the ocean retreating like a defeated army. A vestigial mammalian dream fulfilled; holding imperial vantage on the world below.

The whale felt a tiny diamond of heat within his maw and was pleased as much as he'd ever been in a two-century life—his mermaid was alive. With the last of his remaining strength, he unhinged his jaws to free her.

Muriel sat next to his starboard eye as he watched the sun cross the sky and then the stars come out, all the way until morning. He quivered again as the sky brightened, but a different expulsion was left this time—a boulder of ambergris. Slick and grayish black, the size of a small dog. Worth more than even gold, though enough treasure had been strewn about to feed the island for many years.

A corpulent sun rose through a *caldeirada* of rusty clouds, the plume of hellfire smoke still rising in the distance, drifting off up into the jet stream. Muriel felt his heart stop. The sound of it was something that was not noticed until it ceased. It had always been there. Now it was gone. The iris spasmed, then fixed. Muriel was his lasting image. She gently lowered his eyelid down, closing the curtain, plucking a cockleshell from the crusting to make herself a ring.

🕊

Muriel went blind from parasites and lost her foot from infection, but became the resurrected Goddess of Ciclope. Fed and pampered, anointed with ambergris, festooned with gold by the villagers, who'd regained a lost faith. Or concocted a new one. The little girl, Beatrix, lone survivor from her tourist party, became a sort of lady-in-waiting, a treasured friend, and perhaps, in time, a future Goddess.

The great blue's bones were cleaned and boiled, fastened in the shape of him inside the walls of *Ciclope*, which fit his dimensions perfectly, his huge eye displayed in a block of amber, looking out to sea. Muriel lived within him; the wind through the slats singing his sweet, cetacean song of love. The tale of the mermaid and her whale would always be told.

Muriel Woods was adored for the remainder of her days.

# BLOOD UP

Bunny Hampton closes her eyes, and the promise of imminent mayhem runs lush and electric, rumpling gooseflesh down her arms. Everyone's lost count of how many times it's come to this. When it always seems to, why even hang a number on it? Bunny's a minor legend on this slice of the map. Bringing men to violence is what she's mainly good at.

*Vous demandez des raisons. Ceci est tout ce que je sais.*
(You ask for reasons. This is all I know.)

A crowd grows by the minute in the vacant lot out behind the old Hoquiam Hardware Store. Two powerful, sullen men—Bunny's men—eyeball each other from twenty paces, rolling shoulders in small ovals, cricking necks, and snorting their best bull impressions—all in prelude to pummel/kick/grapple and bite. There will be spitting too and maybe even some eye gouging. Whether it's to go all chivalric defending Bunny's honor, so called, or just to prove their mettle, does not hardly matter; she's conjured this altercation into being and soon will moisten and smile wide as a rainbow. This never fails making strange joy for her in ways the sum of all other pleasures in life cannot come close to.

*J'ai toujours été la fille de papa.*
(I was always a daddy's girl.)

You can't really call it any sort of true evil, and Bunny is victim too of this compulsion in her. Only once has anyone been killed, and that time was plainly accidental, down in the shoe-sucking mud at Moon Island Pier, where halfway into a fairly mediocre fracas, Arnie Brewer rolled off into the dark harbor somehow and stove his head in on a piling. For that, Ricky Thornquist got slapped with manslaughter but served only six months.

Bunny had visited Ricky up in Clallam Bay Corrections, where she quickly began chumming it with another con, a hard case from Wenatchee. She began to rack more visitation with the con than Ricky, which naturally pissed him royal and—just the way she'd have it—sprouted a hellacious beef between the two.

*Mère m'a appris à être une bonne cuisinière.*
(Mother taught me to be a good cook.)

Bunny was habitual, but she knew damn well she'd never get near the yard, the showers, or wherever their rage would be unleashed. When it came time for men to make pulp of one another, Bunny needed proximity—to whiff the musk of the rutting, hear the meat-slap and the low-blow moans, to feel that wave of heat coming off flesh all pocked and streaked with ribbons of fresh welting and scrapage, the blood-slime shaking loose and raining all over when someone finally got a good smack in. She would swoon to the music of their profanity, tumbling out in one long, cascading epithet. All for her. All for her.

*L'école était importante et je me faisais des amis facilement.*
(School was important, and I made friends easily.)

I am one of Bunny's sullen men—a humble jack of several trades, master of nary a one. How have I come to be standing here in the cool salt breeze, ready to get pugnacious with a tower of Croatian sinew belonging to one Josip "Joey" Perkovic? Our Bunny has engineered mutual animosity with precision; of this she is quite sure. To quote the bard Donleavy, "Happiness is a big cat, with a mouse, on a square mile of linoleum," and this sums her machinations well. We are mere playthings dangling from her puppet strings.

A Bazooka-pink balloon grows dangerous between cherried lips, then gets tongue-popped from within and sucked back like dragons' breath. She stands front and center, tarted up and tiptoeing on a small hill of sandbags to better view the carnage we are about to inflict, twitching in her tight capris as if it's *Rebel Without a Cause*.

I'd played ball against a few of the Perkovics, an inbred jock factory across the Wishkaw in Aberdeen that just keeps spitting out the ornery beasts. Little brother Marko was 8-5 back in the wild west of early UFC, but Joey was their star of stars—All-Am at The Dub and starting tight end for the Bengals his rookie season till his cruciate was snapped on a nasty chop block. Even gimpy and winnowed by the years, he is still one certified motherfucker. I've been known to be quite the clever bastard in a street fray, but I'm a good fifty pounds shy of Joey and have lapped the sun a few more times. I've already procured three porterhouse nursemaids, waiting in a cooler nearby to tend the hematomas I know are destined for me post tussle.

*Je faisais les plans de devenir un intellectuel.*
(I made plans to become an intellectual.)

67

I was up eight grand at Muckleshoot last month when I saw her. I didn't even realize it was Bunny till our second night together. She'd whacked her famed red tresses down to nothing and bleached it all porn platinum. I'd only seen her up close on two occasions previous, and on each she was jumping around at a brawl, that waist-length mane leaping too, out of sync with the rest of her—flying up with a life of its own.

Free drinks lubricated our magnetism, and we fell into each other in my comped room. Between our varied carnal bouts hardly a word was said. She'd puff her long brown cigarettes, looking haughty on my arm as I tripled my stakes, then haughtier still as I flushed it all down the rabbit hole, trying to exert will over chance.

When we finally offered up our names, a holy-fuck mantra began in my head that should have been a mighty lust-kill, but back in Grays Harbor I could never resist when she'd drop by my cabin, middle of the night. No man could. That Bardot pout and those Deneuve stems shimmied into my life right out of some vintage stroke rag and left me a pile of so much man-putty.

Bunny started a stream of ribald texting meant for hair-trigger Joey, her beau of the month, to discover, and sent taboo messages to me on his machine. Though I tend to maintain an even strain, this time I went AWOL on all things sane—and Joey, well, he was born borderline, so trouble was on its way. It all built like a bolero to this night's mano a mano.

*Un jour deux garçons se sont battus pour moi.*
*C'était d' une poésie incommensurable.*
(One day two boys battled for me. It was a poetry unfathomable.)

Many have tried to pop-shrink the why of Bunny's behavior. Clyde Tucker's cousin knew her growing up and said her family was normal as any Rockwell. Her real given is Jeannotte-Ghislaine Archambault. Dad was some tech tycoon from Lyon came over on business in the '80s and grew to love the rain. Mom was fifth-gen Oregonian. Till she was seventeen Bunny led a bubble life of suburban coddled ease south of Portland in Lake Oswego. No one remembers any soul-fucking incident in her early years. Nothing to warrant aberration.

*Un interrupteur était ajouté à mon identité de reptile. J'étais foutu....*
(A switch was thrown in my reptilian id. I was gone....)

She went off to that hippie school in Oly intent on studying feminist semiotics, but instead started slinking around the local dive bars wearing too much blue eye shadow, trolling trouble, and found that much more to her liking. When she drifts through time to time, she's clearly just a tourist, not a denizen of this side of the so-called tracks. The working class manner she feigns is generally a piss-poor mélange of Hollywood clichés. Which is not to say it can't blur some poor mullet's radar when he's had himself a tank full and she's done herself up wicked with her retro gum snap and that always timeless figure.

*Je me languissais d'être une mauvaise fille.*
*Une sorcière, une escroc, une Shangrila...*
(I hungered to be a bad girl. A witch, a trickster, a Shangri-La...)

We dead eye the other, Joey and I. He's all steel now, psyching himself into the zone. Our throats raw from so many fuck-you-toos, we've ceased verbiage. I look for illicit weight being slipped in his ham hocks as his brothers wrap them. I know I have dime rolls in mine. You can hear the murmur of the odds makers and bet placers, and it's 6 to 3 against me. But I hold an ace or two. My old man taught me cheats he learned from his old man, and so on, and so on. It's deep in the blood here, foolish battles.

Most of last century our neck of the woods here was known as a Sin City, second to none. Riddled with lumberjacks, harlots, and assorted nautical misfits, it was a realm in which the devil himself would walk the straight and narrow so as not to get his hairy red ass kicked.

Out in the Doug firs you can still find the rotting shell of an infamous barrelhouse, The Spar, where on any heyday night the needle grid of a tree-topper's calk boot would surely imprint some choke setter's face, leaving the honored badge of logger's smallpox. My gramps was a blockhead Swedish king there upon a time. The Spar was renowned for the wooden trough under the lip of the bar where if so inclined, a man's kidneys, having transmuted Rainer to hot piss, could just let flow then and there, bellied up, without any bother of a trip to the privy. It would never fail that some poor fool would be sent skull first down that sour sluice at the end of a melee.

*Dans le miroir je suis devenu une autre.*
*Une voix differente était dans ma gorge.*
(In the mirror I became another. A different voice was in my throat.)

You could say that Bunny Hampton is a one-woman revival of some lost primal art, stamped into our helix back in the late Pleistocene when matriarchal ape gals, the ones with both hirsute attraction and a clever noggin, would manipulate the best of the would-be alpha boys to war over them, inventing most of Krav Maga in the process and cleansing the gene pool.

*Les hommes attrappent la fièvre. Je les aveugle.*
(Men get a fever. I blind them.)

Bunny honed her dark skills at car rallies and bowling alleys, anywhere the male of a certain tattooed species might be strutting their beer gut plumage. She could always find two boys ready to hate each other and seemed to know innately which men were more fearful of backing down than walking forward into the velocity of a haymaker.

It was peculiar, though, that rivals never seemed to direct any of their anger her way. She escaped that wrath almost always.

*Peint—je pivote, sashay. Je chante en cadence et nasille.*
(Painted, I swivel, sashay. I lilt and twang.)

Lately it's been rare Bunny can manipulate two hometown lads into any decent dust-up. She walks into a watering hole here trailing that rep shadow, and there's a wisdom now, a red flag that signals let this one go. So when her itch needs scratching, it's been a random trucker passing through on the 101 versus some sneezeguard salesman down at the HoJo with too much watered Jack in him. Both wishing for some long-forgotten inkling of what it means to be a man.

But tonight Joey and I bestow the coup de grace she's always sought—a title fight of local legends. One for the ages.

*Qui sait ce que nous sommes vraiment et pourquoi.*
(Who knows why and what we really are.)

*Here we are now, entertain us,* a native son crooned not so long ago. Without a bell or a Buffer—it begins. We circle and circle back. I think Joey may have a blade tucked in his belt behind him, so I drop to take-down level and rhino my brow in his gut, splaying him flat on his keister. Turns out he has and pulls out a length of silver slick with his own red where it's sliced him—so much so it slips his grip, and as he goes searching in the dirt, I lift his chin heavenward with my steel toe.

"Been with her every Tuesday since Easter, asshole!" I bellow as he blacks out limp for a moment. "You stay the fuck down!"

Bunny is panting from the testosterone chaos she's wrought once again. Her grin is mad, her eyes wide—sky-high over our donnybrook as Joey slowly pulls his six-six frame off the ground to make ready for more. You would think I'd swing the toe again and do it quick, before the world comes all the way back to him, but I do not.

"Hell you ever had her," says Joey, spitting crimson. "She swears on it! And my Ruthie don't never lie!"

"You fuckin' keep away from Ruthie Dellis!" I yell, "Ruthie's mine now!"

Ruthie Dellis, a powerlifter we both know from down at the gym, steps into the light. She's a good six feet, flat-footed, and is ripped six ways from Sunday.

"I'll take the one left standing," says Ruthie.

Bunny double takes, and that cocky grin begins to wither. She just can't fathom we're not fighting over her and moves to face-up Ruthie. The Croat and I exchange a smile and back away as the crowd, savvy to the game on, begins to encircle the two women, pressing them on into violence. There's no one here who doesn't relish a rare display of distaff fisticuffs.

Bunny's gone blind with embarrassment now, which only fuels it worse. There's some laughter, but she hears a hallelujah choir of ridicule as the control she always wields is yanked inside out. She utters things in French, but no one has a clue as to what she's saying.

On the outskirts of the eggers-on, where she cannot see us, Joey and I put arms around the other all brotherly. I rip a length of my shirt to wrap his hand. We've conspired to play the clever one against herself for once, and have sold it well in the flesh.

When we first found out about the other, we raged all ferocious, trapped in the möbius loop of blind machismo. But end of the day, we found much common ground between us. When your scar tissue has its own scar tissue, and there are jagged spurs on broken things you can't remember, you begin to lose some rage. So foolish battles we leave now to younger bones. We're not alphas anymore.

As the Perkovic clan gathers round, back patting and raising brews to toast us, the murmuring of new betting ricochets around the crowd. It's 10 to 1 against the little Frenchie, though she's got her fur up and is screaming like a banshee. What is further known to only some is this—Ruthie's put shards of broken glass and crumpled razor blades in her own beehive, the way the 8 ball chicks roll, so when Bunny goes to snatch hair, and she surely will, those paws'll get cut up plenty.

Bunny is the first to charge, but Ruthie will surely be the last to land blows. And there will be many.

*On ne peut seulement rester qu'un temps le spectateur*
*de ce qui nous passsionne.*
(One can only remain a spectator for so long in what thrills us.)

# ESCHAROTOMY

An hour after sunrise Audrey Higgins hikes up a wounded hill using deep ruts left by mountain bikes to guide her. The whole of the world here is scar now—a county-sized fresh burn in the Siskiyous, where black and gray have vanquished all of green and brown. The last smolderings were mercifully snuffed yesterday by the rain, but only a teasing, just enough to paint ash onto the soil with its weight.

Audrey's park ranger uniform is sweat soaked and chafing raw. She looks back down the hill at her broken line of footprints. She doesn't wish to spook the man she seeks, having already been to the moonscapes of three other major wildfires this summer, missing him each time.

Audrey began climbing at first light and has seen things in the fog that shuddered her—some fur-bearing animal family, a clot of five of them at least, all fused together, teeth bright against glistening sinew, black as obsidian. Fossils not yet a day old. The chemical rot of them burrowed deep in her nostrils and would not leave. Across the way a deer was running blind, unable to steady its pell-mell descent, tumbling down the steep incline until its bones were bashed to powder. Through the chiaroscuro of the mist it had not seemed real to her, the sound of the fall and bleating delayed, disconnected from the sight of it.

Audrey finally crests the ridge, stepping just above the fog line into a vista wide and clear. She doubles over for air, looking out across the other hilltop islands in a rumpled cotton sea, stillness the equal of any horse latitude. She sees movement in the landscape, what appears to be a human figure moving on the next ridge and takes better view through binoculars.

Silhouetted against the low sun, Audrey finds the shape of someone garbed in flowing white. She knows the man she's looking for ventures to places where fire no longer lives, that he prefers areas of immense destruction, blackened to every horizon. Surely this must be Winslow Fulgert.

A plaintive sound floats on the wind between them. She scans with field glasses to find a small bear cub valiantly trying to crawl out from under its mother, a massive beast heaving, near death. It appears she must have dug a boulder up, then cradled her child beneath her girth as the flame tsunami laid utter waste to this ancient forest, but now she has left her little one entombed.

Audrey watches the man wield a thick branch to leverage the dying bear's torso just enough for her cub to squeeze through. It scurries off, yipping and twisting from the harsh caress of wind on tender skin. A lumpen brown thing, only half its fur remains. The man holds out what looks like pemmican. The little one sniffs—approaches, retreats—then eats from the ground when a piece is tossed there.

A cloud glides across the sun, and harsh backlight subsides long enough for Audrey to better observe the man—the mortified flesh, the sorrow. What she can see of him uncovered is rough, mottled scar tissue head to toe. She watches him draw liquid from an ampoule into a large syringe, injecting it into the mother's flank in several places; moments later her writhing lessens.

The man strokes what is left of bear, gently, where ears had been.

A year earlier, in the same northern California hospital where she was born, Audrey had waited for her mother to die. She breathed shallow in uneasy sleep, then moaned awake from bone pain.

Audrey had waved the nurse from the room, gesturing for privacy, but in truth to untap a tiny extra dose on the morphine drip for her mother's relief. Inflicted pain had long been a game of quid pro quo between them, but Audrey no longer reciprocated—her mother had won.

Delicate and diminutive even in health, she'd been winnowed to a fragile husk by disease. Audrey could still observe their common features—skin the hue of milk tea, without blemish, and blue-black hair. Audrey wore hers long, unkempt; her mother's was always coiled upon her head. Both had wide-spaced dark eyes and tiny teeth in perfect rows, immune to sugar and stain. If not for the prominence of their chins, they could have been classic beauties in some bygone era.

"Chowchilla—you were just a girl. You won't remember," her mother whispered, unable to look Audrey eye to eye.

"How could I forget? You made a scrapbook of it. You laminated everything," Audrey said, expecting more of the usual inchoate bab-ble, but whatever her mother wished to say this time seemed differ-ent. She strained to rise; she hadn't given up.

"Down in that church basement—it wasn't what—that man—you need to know this, Audrey," she'd said, finally aiming pupils point-blank at her only child. Audrey listened, her mother's words barely audible above the music of the monitoring machines. Such was the weight of the secret imparted—the Earth stopped rotation, then spun the other way. No one in the world noticed but Audrey. Her mother's mouth held open, a last word stranded in her throat, lips bluing around it. Audrey looked for a soul floating, some ethereal ash rising from her extinguished flame, but there was nothing. Only the silent explosion of what had been said.

As every red digit in the room began to plummet, a flock of white-coats bustled in to peck at her, attempting one more resuscitation. A doctor gently tugged Audrey's arm.

"She may pull through. We'll do our best," he'd said.

"She could never wake and face me now," Audrey told him. "She's all the way dead this time."

On the scorched hillside, a low sound wells from deep within the mother bear, begging for an end.

Audrey tries to imagine the inferno that roared through this forest only hours ago—racing faster than any creature could run, pitch exploding like dynamite, oxygen devoured so quickly gale-force winds howled in to fill the void. Panic and pain in every living thing.

The man takes a long blade from a sheath, raising it high, two-handed, then brings it down in one swift motion—embedding it deep into the bear's medulla. A gasp flies from Audrey, and the sound carries on the breeze. The man stills for a moment, waiting for another hearing of it. She hushes, trying to flatten out behind the rocks.

The bear lies peaceful now.

After her mother's passing, Audrey had been a statue slowly breathing for more days than she could count. There were liens against the house and all its contents, and there was a hole in the world where her mother had been. But equal to any loss was an alien freedom. The last thread of neurotic tether between the two had been severed. Audrey had a will of her own—first time in her life.

She made plans to leave the urn atop Mount Shasta or maybe somewhere in Yosemite, but she'd never followed through. On what would have been her mother's birthday, Audrey started to pour the ashes in the back of the hearth, by which they both loved to read by firelight—then changed her mind, dumping them in the microwave with newspaper clippings of the trial, Church Pervert Gets Twenty. She'd set all of it on *frozen meal*, then hesitated and gathered up her mother's best silverware, the gold and pearled things she'd squirreled away. Audrey stacked those upon the pile and pushed the button, then stood back listening to the hum, waiting for some kind of theater inside the little window. It had begun to fritz—then screamed at the molecular level. Blue electric light danced all around until Audrey thought it might blind her. The mass absorbed itself, congealed by some forbidden alchemy into a ghastly, throbbing pool. Fuses were blown out beyond repair, and a killing metallic stench hung in the kitchen air.

It had been worth it.

The man finishes building a makeshift cabin from half-charred logs of ponderosa pine. Audrey removes the ill-fitting uniform top and begins to pick at threading around a patch that reads Joan Stevens. She stops, then smooths it back in place. How would he even know this is not, in fact, her uniform?

Horntail wasps have come from far and wide, following the olfactory beacon of the smoke to lay their eggs in the roots of dead trees, and the valley buzzes with their sound. A herd of bruised nimbuses in the east promise more rain, but they are liars, all of them.

Audrey yawns, unfurling from her crouch against a warm slab of granite. She lets the afternoon sun rest full upon her face, and enjoys the glow and drift of phosphenes on the screens of her eyelids when she scrunches them tight. Lactic acid from the climb and the drone of the wasps begin to lull her toward the flutter of a deep REM nap. The long journey has brought her to this spot, this moment, here atop a singed mountain. Resolution, perhaps even redemption close at hand, she drifts off into the languor of dream. Then by some limbic gnosis, danger screams back across that threshold. She finds herself wide awake and bolting up—alert to the crackle of flame.

Searching through the lenses Audrey finds the little bear circling the remains of its mother, burning now inside a pyre the man has set so as not to let scavengers desecrate her body. A column of smoke drifts Audrey's way. The cub sniffs its way back toward more pemmican. The man is patient, allowing the bear-child to make up its own mind to come to him—finally trusting enough to let him slather something onto the crimson parts of its skin. Audrey can only hope he will understand what she has come to tell him.

He enters the cabin with a sleeping bag and the sustenance taken from the mother's carcass. Audrey licks the last morsels of the snack she'd bought at a rest stop back in Kirby and heads down the hill toward the soul whose Tarot was tossed with hers so long ago.

🕊

Audrey had hired an ex-cop investigator who wanted five hundred dollars a day to start. She thought him handsome, in a slightly menacing way. Her mother would have loathed everything about him— the wild thatch peekabooing from the V of his open shirt, his brisk cologne, and shoes with heels cheating his height up an inch or two.

"Find the man who never ruined my life," she'd told him, and went on all about Chowchilla, the whole sorry thing, then the revelation of her mother's deathbed reversal. One life had been lived, now another must begin. Audrey had amends to make. Nothing mattered more.

Money was one of many things she'd been left without, and Audrey learned a new currency when it was offered—sexing the investigator for the fee. It would have been an impossibility before the unpeeling of the lies, but now all carnal bets were off.

The investigator had kissed her softly, then harder, and she had let him. At first, like always, she was struck numb by intimacy, out beyond her skin somewhere, exiled in guilt, still hearing Mother in her head—*That man stole everything from you, Audrey; he crippled you!* Slowly, expertly, the investigator brought her flesh alive, and Audrey felt a glow rise down at the crux of her, cascading up her spine. For the first time she understood the wet purpose of it all, what everyone who was normal must have always known about, and she had begun to scream.

❧

Audrey climbs toward the charred cabin, kicking up puffs of ash with each step, whistling "Stardust" to give the man ample notice of her approach. She marvels at the timbers in the structure he's built—all shiny-black, shimmering and shrunken along the grain line. He stays hidden as she sits on a burnt stump a few feet outside the opening. The sun sinks through the marine layer in the west. She says she's heard from other rangers he is a sort of hermit, good with the injured of the habitat, and that he might be staying awhile to help out.

After a lengthy silence, the man begins to speak in a soft, cracked whisper that transfixes Audrey, telling her about his drums of aloe vera, how it helps to heal the wildlife. He makes salves and unguents of his own design for similar purpose. He is always surprised at how many miracles there are to be found—the brave ones who made it through the maelstrom. The impossible courage of the spring regrowth gives him solace. You just can't keep life down for long; it will always find a way to rise again.

He says the main animal rescue units are all off working the other side of Wagner Butte—the fire having finished itself out that way. There would be livestock to wrangle back into remnants of incinerated paddocks, and many volunteers pitching in. He chooses the remote acres, and the wild ones left on their own, some with the fear and cunning starved out of them. Helpless children who need a soothing hand.

A window opens in the clouds, and Audrey is allowed a better gaze upon him—a flash of his moon-textured skin, the lonely color of his eyes. Against the endless gray around them, they seem too blue to be human. With the sun reveiled, he disappears again in shadows.

He tells more of fire, how it is all part of the grand holistic plan. Hundred-year conflagrations are the only way to birth certain necessary seeds. Nature can be harsh sometimes, but it is always wise. Grace in destruction. To behold five-story flame is a wondrous thing— a golden cathedral rising to heaven, the heat like God wrapping his loving arms around you.

It had taken only a day and a half for the investigator to track down what Audrey needed.

"Damn internet!" he'd coughed. "Used to be good for two weeks' shoe leather finding out this shit. Now it's all right there for everybody and his brother."

He told her all about the man she was looking for. His name was Winslow Fulgert. Her testimony about Chowchilla had sent him away for twelve long years. Later, when he'd been paroled to the small town of Boon, Idaho, he'd been burned by an angry mob. They found him guilty of mere existence in their neighborhood, on a list named for someone's daughter, and they had set him on fire. Regular, normal people.

They set this man on fire—over her.

Audrey steps closer to the burnt doorway, asking if he would like to hear some music as she takes out a portable unit from her pack. He would like that very much, he says. She plays him sad pieces she discovered working at a college radio station in Oroville two summers ago: the sighing guitars of "Albatross" from the Peter Green days of Fleetwood Mac, the melancholy crescendos of Godspeed You! Black Emperor, and several aching fado ballads. They lilt out over the pristine desolation.

She tells him about her father, who abandoned the family a week after Audrey's birth. He was from Coimbra, and maybe that is why these ballads grip her heart so. Once, when she'd tried to play them at home, her mother had poured wine on the boom box and thrown it out the window, banishing them forever from their household. It only made Audrey love them more.

Audrey tells him many other lands have some equivalent term for *saudade*, what the Portuguese call the sweet despair of life—an impossible yearning. The Dutch call it *weemoed*; the Welsh *hiraeth*; Finns *kaiho*; Turks *hüzün*; Italians *malinconia*. She sings along, her tremulous voice breaking.

> *If when saying goodbye to life,*
> *a gull would come—*
> *bring me Lisboa sky.*
> *And in that sky is a wing not free—*
> *a wing that cannot fly,*
> *it weakens to fall upon the sea.*

Even if clouds won't give up their tears, Audrey is sure the man is crying in there somewhere, listening as batteries drain, the melody slurring down.

🕊

Audrey had ventured out to Boon, Idaho, and found that old neighborhood. Half the people had moved away since that black day. More each time Court TV ran the reenactment, under the banner, *Neighborhood Vigilantes, Could You Turn into One?*

There had been quite a throng that afternoon, the newspapers said. A throng. It was only a vocal few at first, then others had given into the wicked sum of it. The madness of crowds. Someone poured gasoline. Matches were tossed. Fulgert had whooshed up like a barbecue igniting—flailing and spinning, moaning a blue streak at the lot of them as most had cheered. Even some children were witness, laughing at the fiercest clown anyone could ever imagine. One brave family finally rolled Fulgert on the ground with a sleeping bag to smother the flames. By then he was within an inch of his life.

That same family, the Moothardts, had gone to the hospital for a while, but though Fulgert never said much to them, over the years they would get letters from him with photos of fresh-quashed western wildfires—Nestucca Gap, The Marble Cone , East Great Forks. They'd given Audrey some to aid her search.

"Did you know he was burned once before that mob did what they done?" Mr. Moothardt had asked. "Head to toe. When he was young. Some say it was a truck crash on The Grapevine. That he'd tried to rescue a girl trapped inside but couldn't save her. Others say he made all that up, that he done it to himself just cause he thought he was too pretty for a boy. Nobody knows for sure. But that's what saved him, that old scar tissue. Twice as tough as normal skin. Saved him from a certain death. Winslow Fulgert—burned twice, he was."

🐦

Returning from a nature call, Audrey finds a canteen cup left on the stump, steaming in the mountain air. She sips and begins to feel the narcotic charge of the elixir he's mixed for her—hot blood drained from the mother bear spiked with grain alcohol, peppered and salted, the kick of ursine adrenaline and endorphins still laced thick within it. As the Latgawas of this region would have done, he's harvested the productive parts of the mother. It is not in any way a sacrilege; it honors her. The gallbladder alone, sold to an Asian apothecary, will pay for a hundred morphine doses for the poor victims of future catastrophe, he tells her.

The sun eases into the horizon, and temperature quickly plummets in its wake; the moonless night steals the sight of everything. The man has begun to stoke a small fire, and Audrey is drawn inside by the welcome of its warmth. They both know she has nowhere else to go. She enters his realm, trying not to even think his name inside her head, fearing he might hear it and know why she has come, though she is no longer truly sure herself.

They talk until his voice is spent, aching from the strain of rare conversation as much from smoke and ash. He tends the fire, and the hardened claw of his hand brushes her skin as tenderly as she's ever been touched. He disrobes and lathers himself with ointments, letting Audrey smear his back where he cannot reach—sweet vapors mixing surprisingly well with acrid sulfur and carbon on the breeze. As her palms slide over the sharp ridges of his reptilian form, she tries to imagine what it would feel like to slither over him as a good lizard would. When she gently alters the intent of her hands just beyond a healing gesture, he resists the overture. He could have her right now, Audrey thinks; yet he declines.

Later, as embers die and they cling together for necessary heat, her skin scrapes raw through layers of cotton.

"Didn't bring your ranger gun up here, did you, Joan?" Winslow Fulgert asks, his last words of the night. He goes fast to sleep. She follows an hour later.

When Audrey wakes at dawn, he's gone, and she is, much of her, fresh scab.

Last month, Audrey had volunteered with the cleanup crew at a vast burn site in northeastern Washington state. The forest rangers there all knew some Fulgert lore, though only two had ever actually seen him. He was legend, like the sasquatch or chupacabra. One dubbed him The Gator; another called him Ghost Toast. All believed he'd show up on the Oregon coast once they had containment on the hellacious Siskiyou fire down there.

Later that day, the men were trying to get the goat of a female ranger.

"Hey, Joanie. You know how you get rid o' your crabs? Shave half your pubes, light the other half on fire, and when they come runnin' out, you stab 'em with a fork," the chief had joked, and everyone laughed but Joan and Audrey.

An hour later, they had all run off on a hotspot call, and Audrey pilfered the uniform Joan left on her desk, packed in blue, just back from the cleaners. Their sizes were similar, and Joan had confided to Audrey she was on the verge of quitting anyway.

Driving down from Okanogan to the Oregon coast, Audrey had seen the black plume three hundred miles away. The easterly winds dusted her car with thick gray soot. She waited at a motel in Ashland where a power outage had closed down the local Shakespeare Festival, and spent her time leafing through burn and skin disease books by candlelight. Moths circled like planets. What was it like to be caught in flames, feel your flesh afire—to know that you were nothing more than cooking meat? Turning pages, the wounds deep in keratin and squamous, damage done to malphighian layers, all seemed to shimmer alive in the aurum light.

For weeks, hundreds of smokejumpers had worked the countryside. When the rains had finally come, the sky of smoke dissolved to just a dozen wisps, then in a matter of hours, all but a few of even those were gone, lifted off to Greeley and another untamed superfire.

Audrey finds Fulgert's filthy white garb laid out across a boulder, then sees him swimming naked in a small mountain pond. A delicate mist hangs like frosting on the water. She watches him hand-catch a trout, then feed it to the cub. He pulls up another wriggling fish, biting into it himself, his face left speckled with translucent scales.

The cub gambols off as Audrey approaches. Fulgert kicks up sediment to cloud the water and her view of his flesh, hiding in debris swirling on the surface.

"The little one, she's a girl," Fulgert says. "Think she's gonna be just fine, she don't get infected." Audrey moves along the shore as he speaks, trying to keep the low sun from her eyes as it ripples off the pond.

"This water's probably got all kinda cooties and amoebas and all that. Bet you don't know most parasites, they get their start in a snail maybe, then a bird. But people, they're just the third of what should be four stages. That last one, its true fulfillment, can only come about further up the food chain, once it gets itself inside a wolf or a bear or a predatory cat, like a cougar. Primitive man used to get himself eaten by superior creatures on a regular basis. But no more in these modern times. Little demons never get to really bloom."

"I'm not really a ranger," Audrey blurts before he can say more, and Fulgert dips down almost below the surface. "I can't tell you how sorry I am for what they did to you, Winslow."

"Nothin' done I don't deserve," he whispers back.

"Chowchilla," she says and waits for reaction, but there isn't one. "My name is Audrey. Audrey Higgins. They hid me behind that barrier in the courtroom when I testified. You probably couldn't see me."

"The girl in the church basement," he says with flat affect.

"My mother ran the Sunday school there. I just went down to take a nap."

"I was standin' over you when she came in."

"But you didn't really do anything, did you?" Audrey says, peeling off her clothes and wading in up to her knees. She grabs a breath and extends out, gracefully piercing the surface, and comes up trembling. He is gone—then, from the safety of the leaves, he floats up again like the Creature from the Black Lagoon, squinting, studying her face.

"Mother told me over and over she'd seen you do things to me. She said it so many times I thought I remembered too. But that was a lie. It was all lies."

Hungry minnows nibble at her bright scabs; blood flowers in the crystal water.

"Watched you for the longest time. You giggled in your sleep. Someone told me there was a little Downs gal that stayed there sometimes. All I found was you."

She swims toward him, but he paddles away, just beyond her reach, leading her out into deeper waters.

"And you never did those things they said."

He stops and lets her drift near.

On the horizon, a skein of Canada geese glides through the dawn clouds, their honking serene, a calliope in the sky. As exquisite as anything Audrey has ever witnessed. All that is right and natural in the world.

For a long moment, he's vanished again—then rises up point-blank in front of her. In the hard light there is nothing left for imagination, no choice but to behold the living wound of him; yet his eyes, their cerulean still pure and luminous as the day he came into this world.

"You were a normal girl. Didn't want you like that."

"And now?"

Treading water has fatigued her. She eases into his arms, and he keeps them both afloat.

Wind jangles the last leaves of the weeping spruce. He gazes up at the perfect V of geese.

"Look at them, Audrey. Those birds. How do they keep that shape up there like that?"

"And me—now—Winslow?"

He whispers in her ear. She can choose—he wants her to choose. Winslow pulls Audrey under, dragging them both below. The surface falls away. Gold light on the leaves fades dull brown in the depths. The wavering image of the geese passing overhead is the last thing she may ever see. Drifting down to the dim bottom, another silent explosion builds in her lungs.

Life has come to this. An acorn fallen to the bottom of a lake. Unsprouted. Unloved. Unlived. All she can fathom as she fades is— passion bests everything she's known before.

Audrey spits out a vow that floats away in a warbling globe, a soul rising to heaven. Yes. She says yes. Winslow kisses her, feeding her a saving breath of his own dying air, and pushes hard in the silt to propel them back toward the world above.

They rise—into a life together.

🐦

"Hold your lips tight now, sweet Audrey. Nostrils too. Lungs are key. Gotta keep 'em safe. You'll need 'em. Now put the goggles on."

A month later, Audrey and Winslow are alone in what's left of another spent forest, high in the Sierras, fifty miles from Chowchilla. He has reignited the remains of a four-thousand-year-old bristlecone pine. He smiles at her through a wall of amber-red flame that undulates between them.

"These trees are special. Alive maybe even when Moses walked the earth. Can you believe that? Only you and I will ever understand."

Audrey steps slowly through the blessed fire toward him. Engulfed. Hair gone in an instant. At first she feels nothing, then all at once ten million cells of her are screaming. Winslow extinguishes the golden aura leaping from her. Her born clay glazed anew. Though heavily dosed with opiates, still she goes mad with pain.

When she is ready, he anoints her skin with aloe and the salves known only to him. He tends to her infections with fresh-plucked herbs he's foraged. In time, she heals. Winslow caresses the fresh rough essence of her. Audrey feels him now with shared skin—scar to scar. He gives himself to her. It is all she could ever imagine.

They venture far and wide as nature roars, sharing their mercy with the brave little ones in the aftermath. The next year she steps through the gaping mouth of lovefire again—toward him, her sweet Winslow. He steps through toward her. Every year of their lives. They grow rings like trees.

Moving on to the next dead forest.

# CHRONICLES OF AN UMBRA HOUND

I was born in the year 1943 in the remote Australian outback during the precious moments before Baily's beads. My eyes unopened, I could not witness the splendor of the diamond-ring effect as rays burst through valleys at the edge of the moon—or the hush of the ocher desert bathed in a million acres of lunar shadow. But that does not negate that it changed my life forever.

Mother never took her eyes from the event as she breathed and squeezed exactly as our Sydney physician instructed. Father trained his gaze skyward for the full *seven minutes and twenty-one seconds*, transfixed by the celestial dance taking place a quarter million miles toward the sun. Neither glanced at my tinting-pink, placenta-slathered face until day was given back from false night.

When it was over, they first regarded each other, smiling back confirmation of the other's wonder, then finally looked my bloody way. Both were selfish with their *totality* in a way I have never been.

On more than one occasion I've chosen to gaze into a lover's eyes rather than the heavens above.

The vast shade of the umbra raced off across the land, sliding over Ayers Rock like a spill of India ink, and my parents finally looked to me in the hands of a tsking Perth RN, who by then had cleaned away most of mother's obsolete innards. This nurse did not think my folks deserved to cut the umbilical, as they'd been so inattentive to the delivery, but as she started to snip, Father snatched the scissors and did the deed. I did not cry, I am told; in fact, I cooed—an indication I would be well prepared for enduring hardship later in life.

An Aboriginal shaman was intrigued by a birthmark on my neck, to him the shape of the world: Australia. He gave my folks a pale-blue river stone that I have worn around my neck on a kangaroo-leather strap much of my life.

Some believe one's first moments in the world set an indelible stamp on your psyche, and if so, then I have been blessed to be born of great magic, pressed with a holy template. If my squandered life has primarily been only the collection of illusory moments, I cannot regret it. If it is an addiction to wish to stand and let heaven's breath come wafting down to touch softly on your skin and deeply on your soul, then I am addicted, but if it is addiction, it is not a petty one. Egyptians, Babylonians, Druids, and Mayans have pleasured their deities with noble witness of these secret, sacred moments.

And if my reverence is pagan, as my Aunt Greer tried so painfully to convince me, I do not care. A total solar eclipse exists only because the sun's circumference is exactly four hundred times that of the moon, and only because the moon is exactly four hundred times closer than the sun. The impossible celestial mechanics of these three orbs aligning—their *syzygy*—is a divine gift and all the religion I've ever needed. Beholding them has been quite simply, my sole pursuit, to the detriment of any semblance of a so-called normal life.

I was a drooling four-year-old for the great Amazonian eclipse of 1947—*five minutes and thirteen seconds* of sublime totality to be enjoyed among a small elite crowded atop the Teatro Amazonas, an opera house in Manaus, that incongruous little metro dwarfed by the vast Brazilian Rainforest—the uvula in the back of the throat at the mouth of the Amazon.

Magirelle Dostaniene, a duchess of dubious heritage, was the host of this soirée and had picked up the considerable tab to bring south dozens of her ne'er-do-well friends and several eminent scientists. As a Bach fugue rumbled up from the Brobdingnagian pipe organ in the concert hall below, elegant black-tie patrons sipped premium rum and waited for the sun to be eaten over liquid horizon.

All day the *boutu vermelho*, Brazil's pink dolphins, had leapt high in acrobatic formations. I was told later by Professor Phibert, a "Corona Fiend" from Baltimore, that a startling event had taken place earlier: a young dolphin had beached herself next to me as I napped on the bank of the great river. She twitched and squeaked while I slumbered, my eyeballs' REM motion seeming to be in league with her strange voicing pattern. The gathering witnesses swore they saw my blue river stone glowing and pulsing with a subsonic drone as she slipped back into the Amazon. Perhaps these highly evolved creatures understand a planetary crux far better than we. Indeed, their mammalian ancestors once walked the earth in wolf-like form in some lost antediluvian epoch and possessed a vast genetic wisdom we should love to hold council with. (Why had they returned to the sea? What drove them? And will mankind someday face that same fate?)

As the "faux nocturne" approached the opera house, my parents were distracted as usual and left me to wander among a thick forest of legs. I was lost and frightened, expelled more than once from the comforting dark beneath a woman's gown. I remember the Brazilian eclipse for the cacophony of raucous animal chatter that rose before the darkness fell, receding again as Sol returned, much like "the wave" in the sports stadiums of the later century. From a whisper to a scream to a whisper, and along with the empyreal Music of the Spheres—it was an awing thing.

I was eight years old in 1952. My parents, being open-minded and eager to acknowledge all faiths, had hoped to view the *four-minute-and-thirty-seven-second* planetary tawaf at the Great Mosque in Mecca during the hajj, but hiding mother and me in Bedouin garb finally seemed not worth the risk.

Plan B was scuttled as well—an arduous trek to watch from the Tassili Plateau in a most formidable patch of the Libyan Sahara, near the cave paintings of an unknown mushroom cult dating back twenty thousand years. (Father and Mother adhered strictly to convention in their day jobs, banking and Red Cross fundraising respectively, but surprisingly they were also early pioneers, along with Hoffmann and Wasson, of shall we say a certain expanded-consciousness movement. This was never any sort of hedonistic indulgence for them, but strictly an academic, ethno-botanical inquiry. Or so they insisted.)

Alas, arrangement with the matriarchal Tuareg warlords of the area could not be reached in time, so we stood instead amid the throngs at Giza and witnessed what the Egyptians must have been about. Via a trio of pyramids like giant thimbles and a triad of orbs looping in space, you sensed thread being woven into fabric on some cosmic loom, what Yeats called *the cloths of heaven*.

The pinnacle came as the grand "huzzah" of two hundred thousand human voices Dopplered right along with the mammoth silhouette of Luna and the great candle was ever so briefly blown out. As it was for many others, the transcendence of this eclipse was the thing to which I then consciously pledged my life. It was my obsession.

In 1955 I was a sickly eleven-year-old and practically died from the dozen shots needed for our next long trip but was finally up to snuff by the day of the eclipse, which was going to be a *six-minute-and-twenty-three-second* supernal spectacle at Angkor Wat—an ancient temple whose majestic spires protruded up through the densest Cambodian jungle. Our excursion was led by a Tibetan monk, a Kabala scholar and one of the few remaining leaders of the modern Golden Dawn.

My folks always preferred our viewing locations to have a connection to history, believing that this was just as crucial as the sky in giving up great intangible joys. The ecliptic procession at Angkor Wat was magical as always but somewhat subdued, the thick tropical atmosphere dimming the luster, as if we were seeing it through wet gauze.

A tiny Khmer girl took me by the hand just after the event, leading me through nearly impenetrable vegetation to a vantage where we could spy a young English man and woman coupling near a waterfall. We looked into the other's eyes, kissed ever so briefly in imitation, mingling spiced breath of cardamom and galangal—then giggled uncontrollably, irritating the couple. One of them threw a shoe at us, which I would possess for years: a maroon pump, size four. I chased the laughing girl back through the mangroves but lost her somehow. She was my inkling of a primal Eve, and I her glimpse of modern Adam—all as ephemeral as the alignment above had been.

My parents had dinner the next evening with the handsome twosome we'd observed, newlyweds from Cardiff. I blushed deeply, and that dormant wine-stain birthmark erupted on my neck, as it was wont to do in moments of embarrassment.

"Your boy—his eyes tend to wander where they outghtn't. And that blot of his welling up there ... something quite rude about it all," the husband said. My eyes continued to graze the woman with so much mischief I was sent to bed early.

On Hilo, the next year, June 8, there was to be a *four-minute-and-forty-five-second* span of aberrant night. Many totality trackers ventured to the giant monolithic heads of Easter Island, which, cruelly for them, were completely clouded over. Often as the penumbra approaches, there is a sudden cooling flux of micro-weather, which can ruin an otherwise crystal clear viewing day.

We had originally booked Rapa Nui as well but were victims of another sort of storm, a fiscal one, when the new cruise line we had chartered absconded with our money. Hawaii was our fallback and proved to be a splendid one. My folks chose a vantage with volcanic tumult to accompany the astronomical bliss. Kīlauea was erupting violently all week as if in anticipation of the event, and with the oven winds rising off the lava, the chill of the sun being blocked out was even more dynamic, spawning clusters of translucent twisters, spinning like dervishes over the molten rock formations. I was enthralled by elemental forces, large and small—stars and stone—working in strange tandem.

"Virgin rock is being made right here this second, isn't it?" I asked.

"Yes, it is," Father said.

"And our sun is a star, and stars make elements down in their cores too, don't they?

"Uh-huh."

So this is synchronicity, isn't it?"

I will remember forever my parents proudly smiling down at me.

And that was to be my last eclipse for five long years, until a less than stellar *five-minute-and-eleven-second* phenomenon, again in the mid-Atlantic. My parents would be going, but I'd been growing rebellious, and it seemed redundant to go to nearly the same spot again, so impossible brat that I was at the time, I made sure to act up and was punished by being left home.

When they died on the flight returning, I was crushed beyond functioning. No one could get me to speak for months. I am not sure I heard a thing anyone said. I curled in a fetal ball, nearly catatonic. My life would not be turning out any way I had imagined it; this was certain. My innocence and privilege had been broken on the waves just as violently as their Beechcraft Bonanza, and my imperial temperament began its long slow cooling process toward humble grace.

Aunt Greer attempted to raise me the next three volatile years. I learned much from her about how not to live. She was religious, racist, angry, pathetic, and so much worse.

"My purpose in this miserable life I am enduring is to whip, wallop, and wean the Devil and all his trickery from of any trace of your parents' upbringing. When—if—you ever turn twenty-one, you will get the major portion of the meager estate they've left. But until that time you are in my charge, and that is a responsibility I take dead serious. In the end you will be who you will be—but your soul will forever be scarred with these years."

This was not some metaphor alluded; Aunt Greer actually said those words to me. I realized then how very decent, if distant, my folks had been; their actions were sometimes cold, compounded by their detached logic, but intentions regarding me nearly always noble.

Toward the end of this hellish wardship, a new alignment was approaching on the temporal horizon, and I became reconsumed with racking up prime totality again. I pawned my mother's jewels, which Aunt Greer had hidden away under the floorboards, and decided to do my folks proud by blowing the entire windfall on first-class passage to the next eclipse—setting a precedent to which I would always try to adhere.

I know this lifestyle casts me as a shallow, sensation-seeking lout, but in between my extravagant jaunts I have often lived frugally, laboring long at many menial jobs. When I am among the elite at these astronomical gatherings, however, my peers accept me as a dashing eccentric of probable wealth and a certain mystery, though I have never fibbed one iota of any fictional biography. I appear to be just another of the curious rich, the strictly scientific, and the thrill-junkies who all seek out the ideal vantage for these miraculous displays. For the "civilian," one event will usually suffice, a notch to be made on the experience ledger next to swimming with manta rays or climbing a substantial mountain peak. Then there are the true fanatics, who care not one whit for annular and lunar trifles, but can never let any decent solar totality pass without witness, tallying their cumulative sum under the ultimate shade down to the second. This group of diverse insatiables is known by a varied slang: Totality Seekers, Black Sun Mongers, Alignment Freaks, Corona Chasers, Baily's Bead-heads, to list a few monikers.

I am one of these—an Umbra Hound.

The next great astral brushstroke would paint several Old World centers of Europe. Many of the diehards would be able to sit in their own backyards this time, though it was only going to be a miserly *two-minute-and-forty-five-second* cosmic rendezvous. I stayed clear of Paris and the chain-smoking herds of Francophiles around the Eiffel, preferring to experience the amazing tides at Mont-Saint-Michel castle on the Normandy coast. My disregard for holding a locked stare with the evolving sky saved a life that day.

Most observers were somewhere up on the Mont, but I had taken position down in the sands with a few dozen shutterbugs—looking back across the castle toward the planetary confluence. It is a personal peeve of mine that optimal viewing sites are invariably clotted with manic, humorless photographers who believe they can capture on a plate an exalted, living moment that is best etched in memory.

As light grew dim, a little girl of six, neglected by her folks, was swept out in the shallow tidal waters that rushed in faster than the darkness. No one else seemed to notice or hear her faint yelp. I chased after a yellow dress bobbing in the foam—farther out into treacherous depths. I tripped, taking in nearly too much water myself, searching blindly in the monochromatic dusk, which rendered depth of field nil. I groped below the surface and feared she was lost, but as light burst from the edge of the obscured sun, I caught the barest glimpse of yellow just in time. I dove, rose up with her, and somehow brought her back from certain death. By then a crowd had gathered. It swept her off, and I never knew what became of this girl.

Camille, a lovely woman who taught philosophy at the Sorbonne, had also ventured solo to the Mont. She'd witnessed my clumsy act of bravery and proceeded to reward me with several splendid meals and some advanced lessons of the flesh. I attended to the entire curriculum she required. A dash of Kama Sutra, a dollop of de Sade.

One was warned to refrain from imbibing in 1965, month of May— for a sublime *five-minute-and-fifteen-second* duration—since altitude alone could kill you if you should press your luck with exertion. I was twenty-one and utterly invincible in my mind. This total eclipse would tickle the peaks around Machu Picchu in the highest Andes—a return of an eighteen-year Saros cycle to the place of my conception, if I am to believe my parents.

My parents claimed they made me during their seventh eclipse together. Father's seed began in darkness deep inside Mother's womb, there on the exact spot where the Incas once ruled their world. I arrived the next year—into the light—during the Ayers Rock masterpiece of '47. Mother told me this more than once, and as much magic and wonder as I've witnessed in my life, somehow I have always doubted the story. Yet when I hold the river stone to my forehead, where my vestigial pineal gland is curled up in dormancy, I can often conjure up a hyper-real memory of every eclipse I've witnessed—and a few I haven't as well, including the one that heralded my conception.

There was a Chilean woman name Ascención, older, perhaps thirty five, whom I became fascinated with—raven hair; dark, deep-set eyes; and a wicked, full, brimming mouth. I'd seen her in France, where we'd traded lustful glances; but she was with an elderly gentlemen at the time, and I was being schooled by Camille.

At Machu Picchu, she led me to the far edge of the ruins, letting layers of her clothing fall one by one to the frozen ground, pressing her burning mouth to mine in air so chilled every moist, erotic word was exhaled as cloud. Nearing a crescendo of rarified ecstasy, I noticed first a giggle, then a tiny face peeking around a crumbling wall—which, needless to say, aborted our bliss.

I fervently wished to re-sync our lust with the ménage à trois of the astral bodies in the sky above, but she'd have none of it. I watched alone. It was as spectacular as any ever—the vast dark swung down across the jagged, snow-capped ridges. In the thin air, the shell of sky was a rich cobalt blue and the rim of horizon aglow with an aurum hue. The scintillation of the beads was more subdued this time, however, without as much distorting atmosphere, but the angelic wings of the corona were so vivid you felt you could reach out and touch them.

Halfway through, I felt the gentle squeeze of a hand holding mine. I assumed of course it was petite Ascención, till the very end, when I realized just how tiny a hand it was. I looked down at the face of the little pest who'd ruined our tryst. She smiled up at me. I shouted down at her. She didn't react at all at first, which I thought very odd, but then as I continued to loudly chastise, her mood finally changed. She spat at me and fled into the crowd. Why this urchin irked me so I couldn't reason, but it reconfirmed my long-held notion that children were not for me; their chaos was a useless orbit as far as I was concerned.

In 1970, there was to be a *two-minute-and-twenty-eight-second* sweep of lunar shade across the Mayan coast. To secure the cost, I spent the next four years running my own espresso stand in the Pike Place Market of downtown Seattle. Emerald City denizens were just beginning to go mad for designer Joe. I was among the first baristas in the area and was able to stow away a sizable sum from the cash business (along with a side trade of a certain Mendocino herb for customers in the know). I lived on fresh caught fish and daily bread, slept as the night watch on the lower floor of a magic shop. As was my modus operandi, I blew every saved cent to my name on this expedition—no luxury too outré—leaving my future a blank slate.

At Chichén Itzá, I climbed to the top of a three-hundred-foot pyramid that had been rescued from the encroaching jungle. Déjà vu of Angkor Wat. I shared a fine box lunch with an Icelandic widow, and thought I was well on my way to a charming seduction.

"The latest thinking suggests the main activities of the Mayans in their decline were rampant gambling—primarily on death sports— wanton human sacrifice, and overindulgence in psychedelic colonics. Some believe they outdid Rome for decadence. But I contend that we here in the twentieth century will yet top them both." I rambled on about my fascination with their end-time predictions in the *Dres-*

den *Codex*, but when I realized she had nodded to everything without understanding a single word, the wind fell from my sails.

For this sky opera many clung to the stone steps of the two towering structures. I preferred to look up across them, keeping both framed in my vantage from down on the huge sporting field, which had also recently been resurrected from the undergrowth.

It was quite a spine-quivering sight this time, the presence of ancients felt acutely. Humidity and heat suddenly vanishing as the evanescent gloom swept down from the heavenly rafters. I happened to glance across the length of the field—and there she was, the Brat from Peru. She smiled and skipped toward me until we stood face to face, and handed me a note.

*If you don't talk to me, and I don't mean just a cursory chat—but really, really talk—then I am going to stare at the sun till I go blind!*

Nonsense, I thought. What could this hellion possibly want from me? But as Helios began to be broached by the lunar shield, the girl made good on her dare and looked up, staring right at the blazing crescent. I stepped in front, blocking her view, keeping her in my shade, looking down defiantly for the whole of the eclipse. If she moved, so would I, making sure to keep her eyes obscured. This little dance made the totality seem my longest ever, though in truth it was merely a third of my single greatest. We both looked away to the rippling of the shadow bands as they illuminated the sacred geometry of the Mayan-made mountains, then mercifully blinding gold came cascading down the stone steps and across the field. The world had grown back into normal day, replenishing reality.

I finally took stock of her appearance—eyes fixed in her head a bit too far apart, one ever so slightly crossing. Ears too large and nose a bit too long, but quite aquiline. She had several little snaggleteeth that ruined an otherwise adequate smile. She had sprouted several inches but was still quite awkward in posture and gait, shoulders hunched. You could sense, however, that she might one day grow into her features.

The girl uttered something nearly incoherent, sounding like Demosthenes talking above the ocean with a mouth of pebbles, then made some signifying gestures with her hands.

"You're deaf, are you not?"

"But not dead. Thanks, sir."

"I merely stopped you from seeing stars the rest of your life."

"Icy waters of France."

"Sorry?"

"How my hearing lost."

My spine undulated as it hit me all at once that lives and people had been aligned, not just sun and moon. She was the little girl in the yellow dress I had plucked from the tides. If that was not enough serendipity, I recognized her parents as they approached and shuddered with a second epiphany; they were the same English couple from Angkor Wat. Perhaps I had even witnessed this girl's conception. My brain ached, a fattened sponge with too much revelation to soak up.

"We wish to thank you as well," said the father.

"For your courage that day," her mother said.

"Just luck, to have been there at the right moment," I told them as my dormant rosacea did a Lazarus, boiling up on my neck. If the father noticed, he didn't show it, so I would never know if he remembered those wayward eyes of mine exploring his wife so long ago.

"Africa," said the girl.

"The next big one, yes, in Africa. Are you going?" I asked.

"We are, but..." She pointed at me. "Your skin." Her mother scolded her with a look, then smiled awkwardly at me.

"Your blushing, sir. It is shaped a bit like the dark continent," she said.

"And I always thought it looked like Greenland. From my view in the mirror anyway."

I made a gift to this girl of my custom 20-power solar viewing scope, an inherited treasure that my father said was designed by

J. Norman Lockyer, discoverer of the element helium. It was made of brass and oak with a precision calibrated mirror system and sophisticated smoked-glass filters of the highest grade.

"Please, with my compliments. Save your eyes, young lady."

"Genevieve," she said with a curtsy. "Will treasure always." She fidgeted nervously, beginning to pull apart the delicate instrument, leaving finger smears on the glass.

"Genevieve," I said, bending down, taking her hand in mine—but kissing my own hand, not hers. We all laughed.

In three years there would be a luxurious *seven-minute-and-fourteen-second* sweep smack dab across the Serengeti plains at the height of the annual wildebeest migration—Africa in all its primitive glory under the longest of noonday nights. Once in a lifetime was no exaggeratlon.

In the interim I took on a unique job that allowed me to visit nearly every medium-sized place in the forty-eight contiguous states, with my own hours and no boss—perfect for my prickly nature. It was a side benefit of my minor heroics in France. I'd received a standing offer from the region of Roquefort-sur-Soulzon to work on their behalf, and I finally took them up on it. I was to be one of a handful of their official emissaries in back-road America, protecting the integrity and financial rights of their splendid cheese. I was paid well to eat breakfast, lunch, and dinner in different cafés and diners—both upscale and dive. If the menu stated a choice of Roquefort dressing I asked them to show proof of it really being our official fromage. If not, by law, they were required to pay a fine and change their menu.

My roguish ways persisted as well with a succession of dalliances with this waitress or that, nothing ever approaching even the charade of any real relationship—merely an abacus of sweet memories to be tallied on a long, lonely wire.

I put down a large deposit for early booking with a premier safari company. This event was a must-attend for the buffs and would be the first for many civilians. Professor Phibert, Magirelle Dostaniene and her cabal of eccentrics would attend, along with scientists from all over the world.

I napped upon arrival, trying to shake jet lag from the succession of long flights. Sliced amaganu fruit on my eyelids to protect them, I lay baking in the Kenyan sun, waking to a soft warmth against one palm. Genevieve was sunning in a bikini on the next cot. My hand was on her tummy, palm down, where she had placed it while I slept.

"Got you!" she said. Her speech had greatly improved, with only the barest impediment now. There was a device in each of her ears, which were still too large for her smallish head. Her other features had drifted like continents somehow into a more adult countenance, pleasant, though still incomplete. She hopped up, showed the "hand-print" she'd just captured from me—an alabaster void in the dark tan around it. Human skin as film stock. How clever. She started to run off, then turned back.

"We're all on the same balloon!"

Half the members of our party would be hiking up Kilimanjaro to behold the ninth-of-an-hour extravaganza. We would ride the wind, straddled between the parade of wildlife below and the ageless migration of celestial behemoths above. Some of the wealthiest fanatics booked the Concorde to chase the shadow across the breadth of the continent. This would enable them to remain "in umbra" for over twenty-seven minutes, but for a purist, this was a totality cheat, and being cooped up in a fuselage not at all any plus.

The day before the eclipse there was a five star banquet at our mobile safari compound in the middle of the National Park. After the meal, Genevieve and I walked the perimeter under the endless African sky. We followed an odd chorus of soft moaning to an ultra-secure pen at the edge of the compound. For weeks our Maasai caretakers had tranqed every dangerous beast in the vicinity.

"The Maasai are a fearsome people, never really conquered," she said as I strained to propel her up over the gate. "They marry their entire age group. Did you know that? Each has a dozen lovers and is only one of a dozen for all the others." She laughed at her rhyme. "What do you think of that?"

I crawled up and over by myself, but the blanket we used to cover the razor wire slipped, and I gashed my forearm. "One—the right one—is more than plenty." I spoke clearly so she could read my lips in the dying light, and she smiled in agreement.

"And oh, by the way, good friends call me GV."

Inside, lions, cheetahs, jackals, hyena, wildebeest, baboons, even a hippo all lay together under a canopy of misting pipes. Normally these fierce creatures would be ripping jugulars from one another, but now they panted in short, weakened breaths, eyes glassy and rolling back in their heads—confused by the lapse of their wills. It was a strange enforced peace: a Rousseau world compliments of ketamine.

We waded in among them. The aroma was overpowering, but while pungent, not really at all revolting. It was the breath of Africa—the perfume of prehistory. We lay down against the incredible mass of a regal lion head and held a rousing cub in our arms. We cried. I knew it was probably very wrong to let the little beast lick the blood from my wound, but I could not help it.

It was half an hour later at least—the sky was drained of color and peppered with starlight—when two angry Maasai shooed us out at spear point, and this seemed quite appropriate and all part of the ride.

The next perfect morning, the wind was gentle, rising up from the brutal heat of the grassland. From our gondola we could see ravines carved by a billion hooves over the long continuum of the migration.

The ballet above of planet, moon, and sun, was a bravura pageant and lasted so long you could sense eternity in the gears of it all. The vast cloak came gliding from beyond Kilimanjaro, graying most of the spectrum, yet somehow leaving a dazzling rubicund rainbow in its wake. Baily's beads danced around the black circumference like pearls aflame—the wild Einstein hair of the corona stretched out millions of miles into space. It was the Eye of God winking.

The animals below stopped in their tracks, cowering and howling. Some even taking the sham night as gospel and curling up to sleep. We cried again. Time stood still. Life was affirmed. Everything was possible. Then Genevieve nearly spoiled it with her morbid thought.

"I could die right now and not regret a single thing," she whispered. Her parents and I admonished her for that dour comment, though I had the exact thought myself the very same moment.

We climbed Kilimanjaro in silence the next day. Words weren't always needed between us, and damn few gestures either.

"Back when my tongue betrayed me, my mind was overflowing with things I wished to say. But now that I speak as others do, I am stingy with my words," she told me.

We stuffed our gullets at another supremely decadent feast and said our goodbyes.

In the aftermath, Genevieve sent many lengthy hand-scrawled letters filled with those treasured words, and I returned an occasional postcard. Any alignment between the two of us would be far off on some future calendar page, not now. Besides, I was a proud, stubborn, if stunted purist. I only allowed life to really blossom for me at these totality fests. All else was a Spartan hibernation.

Only after I assured GV that we would absolutely see each other again at the next major eclipse would she let communication fade away. For six long years.

The next major synching of ellipses was to be a near replica of my birthright path. Another Saros reprise that would mark nearly the very same stripe on the world's skin. I found in this an ominous serendipity. GV and I met in Adelaide, where she bought me a sharp fedora and we rode the train out to Alice Springs, boarding a luxury coach from there. Her parents were separated by this time and did not accompany their daughter, now twenty-four. I was thirty-five.

Any modesty and social mores we had clung to before were soon to be flung to the Outback winds.

Genevieve had burst into womanhood in ways I could never have imagined. The hobbled speech and off-kilter features, her slumping posture and loping gait, even those errant teeth—all had grown out of the awkward into something close to perfection.

"You haven't said a thing about how you think I look," she said, but my mind and mouth were not yet properly aligned.

"It's been worth the waiting, GV. Every second of it. I won't attempt any inadequate words.... only that I..." I stammered and trailed off, utterly devoid of anything else to say. She hugged me for this.

All Eclipse Chasers were turned away from climbing Ayers Rock, which had recently been returned to aboriginal control and its true name—Uluru—but my river stone granted us special dispensation, and we were allowed access up a secret winding tunnel carved by a million years of erosion, leading all the way to the summit.

During the *six-minute-and-forty-seven-second* celestial shell-game, we groped in furious union to the didgeridoos droning on the wind. I watched her watch the sky for the entire duration—her pupils opening as the moon slid perfectly into the fit of the noonday sun. Prestidigitation only a deity could perform. I swear I saw a loop prominence dancing on the soft curve of her cornea, washed gold with the great alchemy above. Godhead—pinnacle of my life.

We were now a binary star, caught in the thrall of the other's gravitation, forever locked in the dance of mutual orbit. Or so I said something to that effect. We coupled hungrily again at sunset and throughout the cold night. I left the blue birth stone atop Uluru, returning a gift, I thought, for the one I'd been given in Genevieve—an unwise gesture that perhaps cursed my remaining life in serpentine ways. We walked down at dawn, changed forever.

Emboldened by our tandem power, but hopelessly naïve and unprepared, we embarked on an impromptu walkabout and by all logic should have perished. We wandered lost through the harshest natural desolation, quickly using up food and water. We moved sluggishly in unearthly heat, going quite insane—limping, bleeding, hallucinating. We were visited by local spirits and felt larger gods close at hand, just as Moses and other prophets must have in their delirium, alone in the desert. By the grace of some of these we endured—stumbling into Alice Springs near expiration.

It took us two weeks to heal in ICU. Genevieve wanted commitment. Now and forever. I needed distance again, a reprieve from the bliss of too much life. She still would wrongly assume I was some wealthy, erudite, always interesting person. I was not. She wasn't sure she could take the wait. I was a fool to even test her.

"After all this and all before—and you could walk off in a different direction?"

"Trust me, please, GV, and this is not some test. I only ask for your sake. I won't be going anywhere. I'll be waiting."

I made a decision for the both of us: in three years we would meet at the Taj Mahal, during a *five-minute-and-seventeen-second* evanescence. We would marry and tread a singular path together from there on. But in the interim I thought it best she explored her heart, her skin, infatuations—get any and every temptation out of her system, à la the Amish with their rumspringa. I was older, already sure, and had explored my hedonism to an embarrassing degree. I wanted her to be truly free of any and all regret. To this she reluctantly agreed.

The cushy Roquefort deal had come to an end. But also I developed an increasing sort of vertigo. I would obsessively dwell on motions, large and small—vibrations of the subatomic—the spinning orbs of electron valences—moons around planets—planets around stars—galaxies pinwheeling in space—each one expanding away from all others equally ever since the Big Bang. There could never be such a thing as true stillness. It was a lie. My head would reel, and I'd wake with the room twirling. Travel got to be an issue, particularly over bridges. I would often become unglued and drive hundreds of miles out of my way just to avoid even a short, low-slung one.

It was a bit ironic then that I spent the next few years living like a troll under a huge cantilevered span that straddled the mouth of the Columbia River like a rusted rainbow. I did the books at a Woolworth in the depressed burg of Astoria, Oregon, where I lived gratis in the abandoned top-floor storage space. I wrote obituaries and laid type for the newspaper on the graveyard shift, tried in vain to peddle custom brew, took tickets at the high-school games and sold science kits by mail. These and sundry other small tasks I willingly sold my soul for in order to amass the funds needed to make the Taj Mahal trip in regal flourish.

But what would I do then? Show up at my wedding to soak up more celestial bliss, then tell Genevieve, Oh, by the way, I'm really just an itinerant nobody; my clothes and bearing, everything—all a lie. I realized that if I truly wanted GV forever, if I could ever muster the self-esteem to even allow that possibility, I would need to have substantial enduring means, not just a quick stash to blow.

And so I decided to briefly turn to a life of crime. It would have to be victimless. I had my morals. Nothing too dangerous. I was primarily a coward. But something with a very decent upside. I needed a bundle.

The Japanese economy at this time was roaring Godzilla-like, gobbling up all it wished in its material path, so I moved north and began to service certain illicit fringes of this appetite. First, the quasi-legal harvesting of a huge phallic clam known as a geoduck from select shallows and beaches of lower Puget Sound. I exceeded the limit by several tons and successfully bailed out from this salty, soggy line of work with a small fine and a nice starter nest egg.

In partnership with another digger, Chet Skookum, I left the beach for the deepest forest regions of the Olympic Peninsula farther north and a much more lucrative trade. There was an insanely rare forest mushroom to be found there, worth its weight in plutonium to the Nippon palate—but we would be risking stiffer penalties, since consumption of them by anyone other than an expert could lead to instant liver failure.

Only in the root systems of *thuja plicata*, a nearly extinct red cedar, and only on eastern hillsides in a soil whose pH had been created from the ashes of a hundred-year forest fire, would this delicate phylum even have a chance to exist—an edible eclipse, if you will. It was a hideous alien delicacy, honey-combed like a rotting Elizabethan collar, yellow-black and umber smeared. One finds it where the world is dankest, poking its pubic head up from mulched layers of fetid forgotten matter. Chet and I found an abundance of these anomalous entities.

"We slowly parse these out, and we can truly be rich!" I told him, but after several months of stellar business, Chet tried to renegotiate the agreed upon price. The Japanese middlemen were insulted, and worse, had been watching us. They harvested our entire fungal cache, then turned us in to the authorities. Chet, a full-blood Skykomish and son of their shaman, put a curse on these men—their entire country, in fact. The Japanese economy crashed soon thereafter and still has yet to regain its previous momentum. Coincidence? I think not.

I was arrested, plead out, and was sentenced to several months in state prison. In the lingo of the street, I had "taken the nickel beef stand up" and had not "ratted out" Chet, who felt beholden to me, guilty he was able to weasel away scot-free. I said I would forgive him if he did me one last solid.

"Bury half my share, take the other half and use my passage, my identity, and go to the Taj Mahal. Give Genevieve my letter. Enjoy the eclipse in the style I have already purchased. Just don't try to enjoy my gal."

In the letter I laid bare all truths of who I was and was not. I said I would come to her one way or another as soon as I could, damn the eclipsing of any moon or sun. If she still wanted me, I would be hers, but understood completely if she declined. I would wish her well in that case, hoping we could be friends, and if so I would treasure that always, though only half as much.

Chet was on the New Delhi Express in the wake of a recent monsoon, which had left the world glistening with silver beads. The train whipped around a bend—to find a bus broken down at the bottom of the steep mountain pass. The engineer could do nothing to ease acceleration, hurtling right through it and sending the cars violently off the tracks. They slithered furiously down the hillside without the rule of rails. The clinging top riders flew off like droplets on a wet dog shaking. The train thundered, collapsing upon itself, tumbling over and over—a steel serpent turning on a spit. When it finally stilled, the dust rose a mile in the sky. Any flesh aboard was no longer of the living. What was left of Chet had my ID, my letter—even my fedora.

When I was finally freed of the Graybar Hotel, I pieced together what had happened, and realized my letter had never reached the Taj Mahal. I wondered what GV had thought when I didn't appear. I dug up my split, giving half of it to Chet's family, then in my accustomed style, blew the remaining portion on the next eclipse approaching, which was to be an "ocean only" viewing east of Sri Lanka. A solid *four minutes and eleven seconds.*

Genevieve was not aboard the Royal British Line I booked, though it was her usual. I was still in social retrograde, reticent to feign my old self again after the years of deception, so I remained behind a beard and drab attire, avoiding the Totality Buffs. I was surprised to overhear talk of my demise, and realized word of the locomotive tragedy had spread among my old crowd. Bearing my papers, Chet had taken my identity in death. As an eavesdropper I learned more than I ever wished to know about others' opinions of me, both good and ill.

A cloudbank had threatened all day, but the ocean waves fell to bare rippling at first contact, and the view was pristine as blackest night poured out over quicksilver sea and crimson hovered everywhere on the full-circle horizon. In the cosmic oeuvre of such events, it was the luminous equal of any, and I felt reconnected, made almost whole.

As our vessel came about, we passed close by the vessel from the Royal Danish Line, my usual choice, as both returned home. I raised my 40-power scope and scanned the faces, recognizing several; then, in the very last moment of visibility, I saw Genevieve there at the rail. She held a child, standing next to what appeared to be a husband or at least some serious mate, his arm around her waist. The sun glinted off the Lockyer viewing device I'd given her, which she was training point-blank in my direction. She gasped, nearly fainting from the sight of me. The fog quickly descended, and though I could no longer see her, I could hear her bleating my name above the engine groan. Her glimpse was too ethereal for any credence, and she must have thought I was only a spectral memory that had materialized in the half-light.

I would learn later that Genevieve was absolutely certain I had died on the way to the Taj Mahal. She had traveled to the train wreckage to identify the pieces of Chet's mangled body. My crumpled fedora had persuaded her the gore was mine

I ventured to Lapland in 1990 for a *three-minute-and-forty-two-second* Arctic sky adagio that had its own proscenium of towering neon curtains: the aurora borealis, which shifted through electric hues—green to violet—crackling faintly, undulating like a fifty-mile-high flag to herald the inking-out of our sun.

Genevieve was absent. I had become comfortable enough in my old persona to reestablish friendships with the Totality Gang. Most were relieved to see me walking the Earth again, here among the much too plentiful reindeer. I heard conflicting stories from them: GV was married. To a Count. To a no-account. Happily. Miserably. She lived in Belgium with a Walloon or perhaps in Cardiff with family. Maybe even Malta.

Hawaii was fruitless the next year, clouded out and no word or sign of her. There was another *four minutes and twenty-seven seconds* in the South Atlantic that year. Genevieve wanted to put the phantom she'd seen to the test and dragged her family along to that half-obscured disappointment. She'd taken the Royal British for this one, and even led a boarding party over to the Danish vessel on the chance we'd done another anticipatory switcheroo, but I had remained stateside for this one. She was stunned and thrilled to hear of my resurrection from Professor Phibert, who told her I might be living in Austin or Madison, and that I had been searching the ends of the Earth for her.

Genevieve skipped the next one—a *two-minute-and-eleven-second* planetary tandava, again right through the heart of India—feeling it would be too emotional a déjà vu for her to endure. So did I—same reason.

When a Mongolian *two-minute-and-fifty-second* orbital opus approached, GV booked herself on both prime excursion packages, but when her child took sick, she relinquished those accommodations to stand-by travelers. She had no idea that one of them was me, deciding only at the last second to embark once again to find her.

The Gobi was grandeur unsurpassed, sands shifting like a huge hourglass lying prone, and once again time stood still under the cyclops of heaven. Afterward I shouted her name above the atonal humming of the Tuvan throat singers, but she was not among any of the astral vagabonds at the feast, nor in the camp of luxury yurts, and no one had heard from her in the interim. Everyone was growing old and losing touch. We were all falling into disparate destinies.

I had come to accept that memories would be all I would have of Genevieve. Then, as it was always meant to be, our tangents finally intersected in Galapagos at a *three-minute-forty-seven-second* epic eclipse no true connoisseur could ever miss.

I saw her first, walking over the wind-potted, lichened-covered rocks, the air ripe with guano and sea salt. We stood, staring across an acre of sea turtles basking in the sun. Her visage was unchanged save for the slightest added layer of some voluptuousness and a bit of darkening under her eyes. She ran to me. I walked toward her.

"That was certainly quite a wait, sir."

"There won't ever be another one. I trust you've gotten the devils out of your system, young lady."

And we have not left each other's side since that embrace.

We beheld the celestial mechanics as if they were our first. Darwin was walking among us. The blue-footed boobies took flight, and the equatorial *pengüinos* murmured at the blotting out of day. It was all so rich with history—the pageant of life—and now finally, as the song goes . . . at long last love.

Genevieve had in fact been married. Miserably. Divorced now. Free. Her child, Bettina, all grown, was in fact my own—from our Outback time. Another welcome and unexpected miracle.

All mysteries were explained—my incarceration and death, the circuitous path of the prodigal father and our bedeviled goose-chasing. Anything wrong before was easily righted—forgiven, then forgotten. I was fifty-four. She was forty-two. We had so much wisdom and not one spot of angst left about anything. We were finally properly affixed together in our own constellation.

Our bond was ritualized at Stonehenge on the cusp of the Millennium, during a perfect *two minute and twenty-three seconds* of Dark Age déjà vu. The Corona Chasers, of course, were an integral part of it all, with decadent Druid feasting to be remembered for years. The diamond ring climax of Baily's beads was the ultimate in everyone's memory, exploding above us and holding much longer than mathematics would ever really allow—our wedding gift from the cosmos.

I got to know Bettina, who wrote epic poetry in Latin and played in several indie bands. We made a pact that all of us would never miss another eclipse of any note. The next was another ocean-only, yet like Galapagos, a true natural wonder. It was a strange *four-minute-and-fifty-six-second* aquatic triangulation among a billion spawning eels in the Sargasso Sea. They were writhing and squirming all the way to the horizon—electricity so thick in the atmosphere that ball lightning ricocheted around like infinite pinball.

GV had money, by birth and by marriage. I had none. For years we all lived well near Gramercy Park in the great city of New York, where buildings cloud the sky and life eclipses time. We were part-time docents at the Natural History Museum when not venturing out to witness this wonder or that.

But when evil bisected our new path, everything changed. We were cursed to witness, helpless, that cascading plummet and the urban lahar that seemed as if civilization's urn had toppled over. The awe of it was equal to any—but from the blackest wavelengths of the human spectrum.

We gave up our place to Ground Zero workers, giving them a domicile for the duration of their sacred toil, and GV, Bettina, her boyfriend, and I all moved to the Portuguese archipelago of Madeira three hundred miles off the coast of Morocco. We lived simply—making goat cheese on a stone bluff above the sea in a sixteenth-century compound. Growing old there among the elders. We hiked daily along the intricate levada waterworks, riding the wicker toboggans in Funchal, witnessing every sunset, every dawn, whether mundane or sublime—reading all the books we always wished to. Safe on this moon in the sea, our family grew and branched, intermixing with the island lineage.

We missed a perfect *four-minute-and-fifty-three-second* span of tropical wonder in Madagascar among the lemurs and the bulldozers razing the lemurs' forest. We sat out another *five minute and thirty-two seconds* in northernmost Greenland, where the vast maw of Valhalla bent down to lick the melting glaciers and rival the greatest Fata Morgana ever seen. We were also absent for an all too fleeting *one-minute-and-twenty-seven-second* ecliptic conjunction that bisected the Great Wall Of China as the last dragon swallowed the sun.

Our fellow Totality Chasers visited time to time with photos and stories, but for us, the best of the world had already been seen. My previous imposed solitude seemed so ridiculous now, as did the detours of my testosterone. Family was the only orbit I appreciated. Family was all now.

We grayed, we weakened, we held on somehow—waiting. Eyesight failing, no longer able to walk. We needn't go anywhere for the next Great Eclipse. It would be coming to us.

A *five-minute-and-fifty-one-second* shade behemoth was approaching in time and space, only months away. Family who had left returned to the island. An endless festival began. We were feted for our age, our lives, our love.

As it swept across the ocean toward us, we held on however we could manage, knowing it was the shroud of our Reaper—*that long black cloud comin' down*. We kissed a feeble final kiss, our pupils opened to behold infinity. Life aligned with Afterlife—the passing of the corporeal baton—as Totality took its sweet time caressing us, giving way to beatific expanding light.

Two hearts stopped on the same synced beat, and our melded soul left with that moon shadow, riding the umbra together—forever.

# WOONSOCKET

Henry Collard bussed home from Walpole to Woonsocket at the end of a twelve-year bit to find his son, Jackie, unmoored and graceless, the way a whole generation seemed to be, in constant fidget with the shiny trinkets of the times. His only child had been an eager, clear-eyed boy growing up, wanting to be umpteen things: a goalie or a shortstop; then maybe drums; finally a poker pro, but Jackie no longer possessed a shred of passion for becoming anything. His days now spent being not much more than a depression on the basement couch, a source of sullen, thumb-clicking racket, a sieve for endless Guinness.

"He's floatin' nowheres. A sorry waste o' oxygen. So you teach him, Hank—what yours taught you. He's a Collard. You give him a trade, a life," his ex, Irene, pleaded across the bones of their osso buco for two in the back of Manny's. Like Woonsocket, the restaurant hadn't changed a freckle. Henry had popped the Q here and said the last goodbye before the stretch. His father's wake had filled the banquet room. It was a place for occasions.

"He goes up—you'll curse me."

"I'll curse me too."

They drew sighs and locked their eyes until the tears came.

"Not what no one wished for."

As was his old man Milt and granddad Jack before him, Henry had been the best torch in twenty states—an arsonist's arsonist—the one you called to milk the policy surefire, and there had not been one atom left in the char to ever snare him; only the rat tongue of a partner cost him time.

Despite Irene's blessings, Henry was still not sold. Irene had never brought the boy to see his father behind bars. Made the trip only once herself to ink the split official. But then blood side of family put up a distance; only Collards came round. Those for whom Henry had worked, in the end, stuck by their word. Envelopes appeared when needed. Mortgage paid down as promised. Henry had done his stint in silence, and she began to see him as a man of honor, if only that of thieves.

Henry found his old man's weathered "grail" under a decade's dust in the steeple of boarded-up St. Luke's. A primer bound in hand-tooled leather, chockablock with neatly scrawled notes, formulae, and sketches. A thorough layman's study of various woods and their ignition temps. The proper ratio for the unique accelerants to use for different structures. How to make a timer from a leaking sack of rice, to train a rodent to chew through insulation, then leave the furry accomplice behind in the smolder after a gentle snap of its little neck. A thousand and one other bits of tradecraft.

Jackie cried upon hearing what his pop was willing to do for him. He'd failed at everything he'd tried, and he'd tried so very little.

Father and son set incendiaries together—small houses first, then

116

built up to eight-unit structures. The Collard formula would burn clean without a trace.

Jackie could never get it right; it took beakers and distillery gear, but most of all concentration.

"How 'bout you leave like a meth lab behind at your burn sites? Nobody'd look you sideways these days with those tweaker toys in the ash."

Henry chilled him with a stare.

"Cuz anybody could. This is an art, son. A family trade. You will become master of our skills or you will not go down the Collards' little path in hell."

"I can get it lit, get the hell out in time, just—it escapes me—all the molecules."

"I made enough for thirteen jobs. Freezes okay, but leave room for expansion, whatever you store it in," Henry sighed, knowing the folly to come.

"You can always brew me some more when that's used up, right?" Jackie asked, but never got an answer. The kid would get a baker's dozen chances to become an ace, then be on his bloody own.

Henry could feel his liver quitting on him. Liquids coming out, turning dark. He'd been a sober man the greater part of his living, but toxic work had taken toll. His daddy dead at fifty-three—some malfunction of the blood.

Henry had volunteered to advise for the R.I. Arson Board on difficult cases. It showed those needed showing that he was on the straight and narrow now, but he divulged only a few mundane secrets of the trade. Found half their fire investigator gospel to be sheer malarkey—the myths of concrete spalling and collapsed bedsprings being any proof of pro involvement. Evidence for convictions as often wrong as right.

These buffoons. Henry held the sum of all they could ever beg to know. Would have killed his father, such commiseration. Any opening of your yap to Johnny Law was a sin as grave as any.

There'd never been a question of what Henry was born to do. No collegiate dreams and the like. He'd crawled through foot-square air-shafts at seven, dragging a fuse taped to his cuff, and stood winter lookout on rooftops, Sterno cans upon his toes. Smoked cigars with Patriarca gunsels in Providence social clubs at twelve. Through his teens, he'd practiced craft till he could do it blind and backward. Made the old man proud. Earned the respect of serious people.

Jackie began to work along the Eastern Seaboard. The name Collard still meant something on the grapevine. Began to build a small rep. He knocked up a gal he met in rehab. Not a soul said she wasn't good enough for him. A spring date was set.

When Jackie's crushed and calcined torso was found beneath the support timbers after Manny's burnt down Halloween, Henry's health went fast. Irene caught him set to put the primer to the fireplace flame. She plucked it quick, singeing peach fuzz the length of her arm.

"He left a grandson, Hank. Don't let's be hasty."

# WRAITHS IN SWELTER

**PRITHEE, DO NOT TARRY**

It will never leave her—seven hundred screams melting to a single cry above the roar of combustion. When you've been to hell as a child, you'll always hold some brimstone.

What was little Winnie thinking that crisp Sunday morning, the last of 1903, as she slipped on her rose gown? She'd tried other dresses too, but always came back to the pinkish one. Seven times. Because it was beautiful—and because a numerical demon inside her craved that digit, compelling most everything to be done in sevens.

Her family had wealth, she was fairly certain. Perhaps an inordinate amount. There were a packing plant, a school, and two parks in Chicago named for the Gillespies, not to mention the best steakhouse in ten states. So her clothes were of the finest silk from Siam.

She was off to the matinee premiere of *Mr. Blue Beard* with her aunts, six cousins, and Robbie Temple, the regal nanny who'd raised

Winnie since her father left to set up the mines in Bolivia after her mother perished from a bout of influenza (in truth, a long scourge of laudanum abuse). Robbie, of Cape Verdean Creole heritage, whalers from New Bedford, spoke nine tongues, and she taught Winnie how to use a slide rule from Uncle Isaac's factory in Sheboygan as well as all the standard dictums for *finishing* a proper young lady. Robbie—so proud of her new custom-built Crestomobile Runabout, third off the line and gaudy red as a baboon's ass. As it pulled up, the crowd murmured, assuming surely she was some exotic potentate, layered in her multi-hued finery, hair a grand nimbus of intricate graying curls. Something to behold. The crowd parted as they made their way through the crowded rococo lobby, down the sloping aisle of the parquet level of this three-story cultural cathedral, built to shame all others in the city. Winnie brought her best friend Sabatha, who'd been loved so dearly, stuffing poked from every seam.

Seventh row. Seventh seat from center. Seventh heaven, it would be, she thought, waiting with a tingle of anticipation for the rest of the relatives to arrive and the show to begin. As they all found the Gillespie row and settled in, the star of the play, Eddie Foy, squeezed his boyish face through the curtains, revealing a smear of hubbub behind him, and a little blur of smoke leaked out. He began to calmly announce that there would be a brief delay in the matinee schedule—then something cracked and fell somewhere, and a red dragon of flame ate a hole in the billowing curtain in two bites. The audience, witness to utter chaos backstage, begat their own with a collective gasp, and in an instant ferocious movement flowed toward the lobby.

Because the doors opened inward, they were doomed. Because the European bascule locks of the exits were unfamiliar to these Americans, they were doomed. Because the newfangled "fire proof" asbestos curtain failed to descend; because the Kilfyre containers were half empty (though it would not have mattered by then)—they were doomed. But mostly their fate was sealed as the crowd, reacting to the most primal of stimuli, became a hive mind—limbic and merciless.

The room brightened with an explosion of flame from the stage, then just as quickly began to dim from obsidian smoke. Robbie poured tea from her thermos across a hankie, telling Winnie to drop to her knees and breathe through it. Both were trampled—first by the cousins, then again by dancers leaping from the stage. The aisles jammed quickly; even those scrambling over seatbacks could not move another inch. The stampede stalled as suddenly as it began, squeezing itself into one cruel mass as leaping fire grew everywhere. With her last strength, Robbie was able to heft Winnie up above the smash of bodies, which had begun to cook, flesh melting into flesh. Robbie gave a prayer and a push to usher her young charge on toward the transom above the lobby doors, where arms were waving in a shaft of light. A walk of fifty feet to saving air.

"Forty-nine steps to get there! Seven times seven, little one!"

Winnie froze after taking just a few, till Robbie began to sing: "Skip to my lou, skip to my lou, my darling—"

Winnie squinted back, lucky that smoke obscured Robbie's great head of hair, aflame. The girl could still hear the straining melody through the din and hurried on—as if heads were lily pads and she were a dancing frog. At forty-seven she was yanked upward Rapture-like into oxygen and coolness. A return to the realm of life.

Surgeons all over the Prairie State were called in to delicately sever as best they could the ghastly mass of charred remains for individual burial. (A wicked secret few were privy to: twenty-seven butchers, the best in the city, did the same.) A week of closed-casket wakes and impotent blame, the likes not seen since the O'Leary bovine took the rap for burning the Windy City back down to the sod a score and a half ago.

The *Tribune* caricature artist, Franklin Meeks—fallen back on the sauce again, his cynicism spiking—wielded vengeance against civic fools who'd skimped on safety, against the rich in general, but saved his most acid vilification for a privileged girl. His front-page sketch was reprinted in most every paper in America, prime fodder for a Roman appetite of the grotesque. It depicted a gussied-up brat, doll swinging in hand, as she blithely skipped her way to impossible survival along the tops of human heads—the worst of Bosch and Dore all around her, writhing just below her feet—smiling a carefree, let-them-eat-cake-whilst-they-burn air. Some victims, knowing they would perish, reach up, trying to pull the little imp down to join them in gruesome death. Envy of the greenest hue.

Her name for years to come would engender abnormal scorn. Little Winnie Gillespie—damned to infamy.

### SISYPHEAN NIGHTS

The call has come again from a well-known location, aborting Rahman's knight-to-bishop move. I race my partner to the rack for gear, pulling on an EMS jacket labeled Buddy Rawlson, though that is not my true-born name. We mount the chariot and roar away from Station 43—off through the Chicago summer night.

"Your queen would have been taken in two moves," Rah assures me as the reds are run down Rockwell.

"It certainly would. Laying the Spielmann Trap, my friend," I tell him, and he expels a self-loathing lungful of air. But of course.

It is comforting to know that waiting for us on Windsomer Avenue will be little unknown to be dealt with. A junkie will either be alive or dead. Or somewhere in between. If still breathing, one of us will pump Narcan in their heart and yank them back across the River Styx. If dead, we'll call homicide, cart the corpse, and drown in paperwork the rest of the shift, chalking up another death by misadventure.

It's still the first half of 1995, and we've taken this same call a dozen times now. Over thirty times the last two years. We spew cherry light south, blurring east, then wail up the hill to park at the base of the old Reinhold Arms Building, a stellar exhibit of Prairie

Renaissance splendor fallen to SRO squalor and decay. (One of the few structures in this part of the city to have survived the Great Fire of 1871.) I stop to pluck a handful of red mutant roses from an untended garden, stash them in my bag, then methodically trot the seven flights up. (Otis—deceased since '92).

Rahman's tongue clucks as we rattle/squeak the gurney down the bile-green hall. Wheels were greased again last night but have wills of their own and persist to yelp like violated chipmunks. Faces poke from chained doorways, all the same expression—*not again*!

"Why not let their God take them? You can only tempt him so many times," Rahman ponders, lungs heaving from the climb.

"Took an oath, remember?"

"Then it is we who play God."

"We play Cook County EMS. So says our checks. We do what we can. Go home. Do it again tomorrow."

Mascara melts over mountain-range acne on a once-pretty waif standing in the doorway at the end of the hall, waving us to hurry.

"Iced him in the tub like they said," she shout-whispers, fevered and shivering at the same time, itching furiously at the crook of her elbow. The door swings wide, and out roll the unventilated ethers of those who've lost their shame. Sickly yellow light leaks from windows taped with old Tribunes, peeling in pentimento. Dribbled red caked on the floor from the missing of veins, emptied sugarcrap, and copper scraps scattered everywhere. A couple bodies barely breathing. Rahman and I will check them all before we leave, offer ignored advice and drive away. The slothful monsters we battle here are human will and inertia. They are powerful foes.

Rah repeats scuttlebutt he's heard, that the whole building is owned by Lionel Workman, the bluish occupant we find in a tub of ice. He's held opiate court here for four years now, the last dregs of a once-plump trust fund going up his arm.

"Precisely why you never let your children have a single thing they have not earned," Rahman mutters. "Their most certain ruination."

When I inject the Narcan, Lionel bolts alive like a jump-started corpse in a James Whale film, his body wrought in soul-deep ache as the waif hard-squeezes him with love, nearly back to death again. He nods to her to offer us a tip of soiled money from a cache hidden beneath a rug. We shake our heads *no* as we always have before, but Rahman gives an odd glance, and we both seem to consider it this time. Why the hell not? Next one, perhaps. (As Rah prepped the dose, I'd pilfered what was left of a dime bag from a nodding junkie's palm).

I've been cursed to return again and again to the place my Ruby died, and take this all as penance deserved. Rahman, my partner of two-plus years, doesn't know she was lost in this very apartment. She'd gone to score and never returned. I'd made the Reinhold call three times before putting it all together; such was the state of my life not so long ago. I could harshly judge these addicts, try to exact some hollow Hollywood retribution, but that would not bring Ruby back. She chose the life long before she met me, and I walked it with her for a while. In the half-light and fetid air, I've often thought I've heard her speak my name, turning to witness something shimmering just beyond peripheral view. There—not there. If some limbo-realm could exist on earth, the Reinhold would surely be the place.

In the repetition of this OD run, an ornate door, the only one on the northern side, became a fascination. One could imagine the stellar view this suite must have all the way down Pershing to the Lake. Sometimes a face appeared. At first, just shadow behind the eye peep, but I began to make a point of whistling along with the scratchy 78s bleeding from the mahogany walls. "In the Good Old Summer Time" or "Shine On, Harvest Moon." Noticed delicate foot-steps and soft breathing behind the door. One day, a harmonized humming returned the favor. I came to believe that, upon hearing our siren's slow fade downstairs, the elderly denizen here would be expecting me. Despite Rahman's irritation, I'd often pause to hear the rattle of the chain, the soft click of several locks, and there would appear a sliver of translucent skin and pale cyan eyes, shy and glistening. A once-great beauty, hair oddly coiffed in youthful style from some distant decade. We exchanged smiles, sometimes innocuous chats. She seemed to enjoy my gentlemanly flirting. From the stillness of her room, always kept fifteen degrees below the temp of the hallway, an eerie chill seeped.

She's never let me in.

It became a hobby learning all I could about her. The Workman rumor was dead wrong, though I never told Rah; Winifred Sabel Gillespie owned the Reinhold Arms, as well as six other apartment buildings. She once had a certain notoriety and rarely has left the premises in the entirety of a ninety-nine-year life. Probably a hoarder, said the select few who provided her service. None but doctors allowed beyond the parlor. The super told me there are three redundant AC systems dedicated to her private wing, her cool comfort being one of many obsessions. He gave me clippings—the same perennial rehash article some city rag runs every dozen years or so, speculating about the little survivor of a gruesome Chicago tragedy.

As another emergency call comes in, I knock seven times and leave seven flowers outside the door. (Having learned of her numerical affliction). I do not turn back to witness her reaching out with a walking stick to fetch them. That would be rude, but wrestling the gurney back down the stairwell, I sense a whiff of sweet pollen, and I know somehow her nose is deep in roses.

Any health-fucked soul getting Wagon 19 on their 911 out of 43s should consider themselves a very lucky bastard. Rahman was a fullfledged MD back in Bangladesh. A surgeon, so he says, though he misses a pneumothorax enough for me to doubt this. But he knows his street damage and battle wounds in a masterful way, having used Army Med Corps to snag his green, then become a bona fide citizen. Rah has a special feel for the limbo just before the flesh gives way unto death, as only one who has walked halfway down that tunnel himself can possess. In childhood a congenital heart defect stilled his blood repeatedly, till a Catholic missionary group gifted him an operation. It takes every shred of Bangla will each day for Rahman not to exceed his sanctioned limit as a lowly EMT here in Illinois.

Few know I quit two months short of adding *Doctor* before my real name, and from Johns-fucking-Hop, no less. None know the real story. I've told Rah only that I dropped out first month of a nameless med school, that I just didn't have the stuff and couldn't hack it, not that I'd been on the verge of *first in class* from a top five program. But he suspects what I've hidden; few things escape him.

## CRAZY HAZY KISSES

It had taken only one night veering from the destined tracks for me to annihilate all my parents' dreams. In my previous incarnation—Hubert "Buddy" Kahn—I'd aced everything in life, SATs and MCATs. Phi Beta Kappa Ivy grad at twenty, just waiting out the fait accompli of the next crowning achievement. A five-star banquet of a life was waiting for me—but I went out for a street taco to feed some parasite of self-loathing I had no clue was coiled within me, ready to hijack my will.

Flat Duo Jets were playing Ottobar. Having heard them for the first time, just a random thirty-second snippet on the radio, I went to check their wild groove that night—on whim. I didn't do whim back then. I paid dearly for the deviation.

I met Ruby coming out a men's room stall. A girl unlike all others I'd ever known back in Barstow. *Barstow—the poor man's Bakersfield.* That was another life. Two dentists in the raw Mojave living through their sole progeny—small-town golden boy, class prexy, two sport leagues' MVP, full ride to Princeton. I'd dated Queens of Prom and Harvest there, then courted a few daughters of world industry while a Tiger in New Jersey. None ever sunk the hook like Ruby. She fit none of the folks' criteria for a lady friend. That was precisely the attraction.

She needed a bass player for a gig, the last one, sadly, fresh in the grave. I'd never even heard of a Fender Precision, let alone held one, but I'd been first chair cello up through college. (Same genus, I thought; why not give a try?) It weighed heavy on my neck, and as it throbbed on, crackling out from their stolen Ampeg, my bones awoke. Sine waves surged through my pelvis and rattled thunder in my skull. Her band had attempted rehearsal twice before, but by the second song I was already leaps and bounds better than them all, striving to keep tempo and key. (Which proved pointless). Batting smiles back and forth with incandescent Ruby, I turned my fingers loose, fucked it up and felt the purity and joy of neophyte rock 'n' roll.

I'd never touched a tattooed back. Never lay down with hot inked skin impaled with metal, so ready for whatever. She relished my corruption.

"No rules of desire. Wallow with me, Buddha-Kahn."

Beasts we became. She in heat, and I slave to scent and primal purpose.

I cried when I came. And I came like I'd been birthed again. She laughed at me so sweetly—drinking, toking, hoovering rails of this and that, then Sunday morning, saying, "Church," she brought it out. The needle. So petrified of that spike violating my blue quivering vein. Refused even a skin pop. Mind racing—HIV, embolism, staph. Relenting, I chose to chase the dragon, let an evil wind fill a shallow soul. Possessed that very moment. By the end of the month I followed Ruby to Chi-town as would a yellow chick a mother hen, full well knowing the absolute betrayal being done. Numbed to consequence. So I deserved the hell of '95.

Neither Rahman nor I do angel work just for the money. We do it for some purpose, so the collapsing balloon of our lives won't seem quite as flat. Rahman is a quiet man. The only time he trips loquacious is when we pass one of the creations of his countryman, the Great Fazlur Khan—*Einstein of structural engineering.*

"Chicago is monument to him. There shall always be the Sears Tower—no matter what devil should purchase and try to change its name!"

Rahman has pored over Khan's archives at the Ryerson and Burnham Library. Quotes from memory Fazlur's favorite poet, Rabindranath

Tagore: *Death is not extinguishing the light; it is only putting out the lamp because the dawn has come. Let us not pray to be sheltered from dangers, but to be fearless when facing them.*

His extended family dwells on the entire third floor of a brownstone on Devon. They took down half the walls between units. A bit chancy since they do not own it, but the deed is held by a family who share a business with relatives in Dhaka.

Rahman's social circles and mine hardly overlap, but I've been to his mosque twice, his home thrice. And he brought his daughter Yasmine to see my new band, stayed for two songs and only barely mentioned it a week later. The frenzy of the pit disturbed him more than the speed chording and one-note screaming.

"Not important if we're any good or not. It's catharsis, not even music, really," I explained.

"Some cleansing ritual, then?"

"If you will."

"And the girl you chased from Baltimore, she no longer plays such music?"

Rahman doesn't know that Ruby died at the Reinhold three months after I hit town. That I curled fetal for weeks, trying to stop my heart, but it kept on beating. My lungs would not cease just because I wished them to. The sun rose again and again, despite my damning of the light. When I finally emerged from that necrotic womb of depression and chose to be human again, the EMS trials and tests were a snap. I possessed enough knowledge to become a mechanic of the soft machine, and still had the organic strength of a blue-chip athlete. What better way to pay the rent, as well as procure certain elixirs necessary to remain benumbed, yet highly functioning, when I needed to be.

Khan/Kahn. Would Rahman love the anagrammatical trick of that? Would it offend him? Or only that I'd lied? I appropriated my sobriquet from an old Spike Jones ditty my Grampa sang. Only thing I can remember of him. *Hut-Sut Rawlson on the rillerah and a brawla, brawla sooit.* A staple on the set list of every band I've had. At 180 BPM.

Another serendipity I hold secret from Rahman—Ruby Owings was the black ewe of a founding family of the Great Khan's firm: Skidmore, Owings, & Merrill. They'd allowed the brilliant immigrant's radical "tubular" design to prevail in building the world's tallest building here in the big-shouldered town.

Rahman knows he pushed his eldest son too hard to emulate the Great Kahn. Not just in naming him Fazlur. Nothing short of *Fountainhead*-like prowess in the field of architecture was going to suffice, and Faz was failing, falling further behind each quarter at SAIC. A dowry-sized bribe helped procure a diploma. Another, an internship at SOM.

On his twenty-fifth birthday, Fazlur took his father up to the skeletal top floors of a skyscraper the firm was working on. He pointed up through the naked steel beams to show him the flag-stand edifice he had been part of the design team on. Had, the operative word; the young man was let go earlier that day. Faz knew he would never measure up to his namesake or even a portion of the grand expectations—that he should be designing plans for some future Burj Khalifa or some other noble dream. He noted the limit of his father's patient smile; the sigh upon realizing Faz was merely a flagpole co-designer. As Rahman began yet another lecture about dedication in the land of plenty, his son took steps toward the east, toward Mecca, where no girder existed but on blueprint, and screamed *Forgive me* forty-nine stories down.

Rahman never speaks of this. Only that he lost a beloved eldest son to unnamed disease. But I know at least five variants of the story. Many know versions of mine and Ruby's. Those in the urban fray— cops, fire, and emergency—hold no real secrets from one another; a rumor always will out someday, whispers pass it through permutations until it is no longer the exact story, but still, every word is true.

## THE HEARTH OF JULY

Seventh day of the seventh month—an elephantine weather system ambled in and sat on the toddling town. The wind had vanished somewhere, driven underground, perhaps. Slow, infernal suffocation began. *Cook* Country apropos. Calls were ceaseless once that oven came.

Those who summer elsewhere flew the coop to milder climes, cabins and second homes. Others with lesser means took transpo the hell outa town to stay with cousins and friends, anywhere beyond the red molten lines of the meteorological map. The poor holed up right where they dwelled and waited. They had no other choice. Sleeping on rooftops, sardines squashed into every library and lobby. Toward the end, the day of the killer crux, the enormous power drain of 24/7 AC usage shut down the grid, and it was no longer the twentieth century.

I'd been dreaming of heat after a spring of damp night shifts and was heading west as it began—a quick jaunt out and back via Route 66, burning unused sick days before expiration. The stated goal to spit off the Santa Monica Pier and return posthaste. Perhaps an excuse to find myself passing through Barstow on the way and rationalize a making of whatever amends might be possible. It should have been in a Corvette like Milner and Maharis, but it was a Chevy Citation, which broke down before I hit OKC. Made it back on Greyhound to find the station empty. All of 43s out on calls around the clock, meals taken on the fly. With me not being pegged on the board for duty and with authority so taxed, no one could even take the time to tell me where the hell to go. I helped awhile with the incoming phone jam, but quickly reached my limit of uselessness and commandeered a Wheeled Coach with a broken muffler from motor pool repair, pilfered supplies, and set out to do some fucking good.

Rahman was sleeping the day away after OT on three night shifts. He'd already heard word of the stolen vehicle I was driving, but said nothing, just hopped in. There was no beating anyone to calls, no predatory tow-truck attitude. Jurisdiction meant squat as the city baked. Life moved in molasses. We could not see the burning forest for the ailing tree or two we aided, were less aware of the whole of the event than the millions huddled at the tube, fed the intravenous fear drip round the clock. The news just can't help itself.

If the Reinhold Arms call had chimed, we would not have taken it. There were more pressing needs. But I thought of her the whole time. Winnie Gillespie—all alone in Room 777.

After another thirty straight, Rah became delirious. The plum wine he'd often swig from beneath his seat when he thought I wasn't looking had pulled the water from his cells. He was as high of a functioning alcoholic as I was a weekend dragon monkey, and could hide it just as well. But not in this heat, which broke every deceit upon its anvil.

"It's coming—only miles away now—the great Bhola cyclone," he babbled, believing he was seventeen again and back in East Pakistan.

"Will George Harrison be singing?" I chided.

He wanted to take a kid with a compound fracture to the Royal Empress Hospital on the banks of the Buriganga. It was overwhelming to see such a proud friend come unglued. He looked into me with a father's eyes—at his lost son.

"I'm so sorry—to the depths of my soul. It is I who should have leapt, not you, Fazlur," he stammered, then, eyes clenched, manically quoted his poet till he fell to slumber.

I dropped him home to the anemone arms of his family, all chattering Bengali, in dire need of patriarchal comfort. He took an ice bath, ate his wife's maach bhuna and sabzi, then went back out into the broasting night.

## SOLO IN THE NOONDAY SUN

Anytime temperature and humidity rise toward the century mark, I can relive that peak day as if it were right now. Dormant, folded back in some deep brain recess, easy to rekindle. Eyelids droop, and the day of the crux, when the city broke, waits for me, moment by moment. I am there again.

A hundred and six degrees. Humidity ninety-three percent. All emergency rooms on bypass status. All morgues full. There is nowhere left to go. The belly of my vehicle holds what I believe is perhaps a Kurdish mother, her three heat-prostrated children, unconscious grandfather in renal failure, and two deceased neighbors from Nicaragua.

"Do you know their names?" I ask the living of the dead.

"Always argue. Scream day and night—fuck you hey-zus! Fuck you mah-ree!" the mother spits, unable to conceal contempt.

The oldest child, a green-eyed teen, pulls her mask away, wanting to defend them. "But the next day—" She forms her hands into a vase. "—always flowers."

"Stolen from a neighbor's garden!"

"Then the tears. A squeaking bed."

"And shouting again! Like a clockwork moon, the wax and wane. Madness."

We're crawling through Cicero looking for an underground free clinic I've heard about where one can procure Canuck scrips and such. Perhaps they can take this fragile cargo.

The road ahead is slick with mirage, rippling in heat warp. Someone in a bathrobe stands in the road to block the path, waving a wimple in the air. A nun half-clad in slumber wear. Her body stunted, trapped in juvenile form, though she must be in her late sixties. Sharpei wrinkles looking like a mask, a life of too much sun.

I decide not to run her over.

"A woman upstairs," she pants at the window when I crack it, the hands of Fahrenheit reaching in for my throat.

"Already beyond capacity. Sorry."

"She's going with you," the nun tells me, mouth caked white, fingers affixed round the side mirror so tight I'd have to pry them with a Halligan tool to leave. I offer the last of my water. She waves it off.

"You will drink. And I will take her."

She accepts the bottle, plastic adhering to her tiny trembling hands as she draws a languorous sip of the warm liquid, clouds of my backwashed snot-spit floating there.

"I'm Sister Lucy."

I've heard there are fires now that cannot be put out. Too many hydrants open. This moment I don't care. I crack open one more, in the shade of a distant skyscraper. There's a limp upsurge of a dozen liquid feet, an ever-changing shape, backlit and glowing. If I squint, a human form quivers within it. Today I believe in water sprites.

I pull the wagon beneath the fountain, which crashes mercy across the roof. Metal steams. A staccato beat tattooing, repetition a calming thing. I yank the gurney from the back and roll off to find another half-baked beast for my ark.

Soulless jackals come to pick the ambulance clean of drugs. Hidden by the front end of the ambulance, Sister Lucy pulls her wimple on, the rest of her body still in pj's, feet in bunny slippers. When the vultures assert their way, she pulls out a snub-nosed .38, and they retreat. She wishes she'd kept the bullets, in case it comes to more, but couldn't pull the trigger if it did.

Sister Lucy asks the family if they would like her prayers. They tell her they are Zoroastrian, but they will take what words she will give them. The Sister kneels and gives last rites to the dead Nicaraguans—that they may find a final peace together and never fight again in the next life. The green-eyed child has one more request.

"Can you marry them?" she asks. "They never got around to it. Engaged and broke apart, then planned again, but never enough time between the fights. Could you, please?"

"Of course," Sister Lucy sighs. "And let us hope it will bring Ārmaiti as they approach the Bridge of the Requiter. May we all seek khvarenah—in this life, in the next—unto the last."

The family is nearly turned to stone, astonished by her cursory knowledge of their beliefs. Lucy wishes to ask them if lore of their burial rituals is true—that their heaven or hell is all left to nature's chance. The first vulture landing upon an open-air funeral pyre will always peck first the eyes. If it chooses the right, there is salvation of sorts. The left leaves damnation. The totality of life's good works not factored in. Only a buzzard's whim. Such is eternal fate.

Four flights up in another SRO warehouse of sorrow, a four-hundred-pound woman from Alabam lies facedown on broken tile in the communal bathroom. I tilt her head to expunge vomitus so she won't Jimi out, then strap a mask from a small go-tank, which blesses her with the minimum $O_2$ to keep her this side of the Pearly Gates for a while. Neighbors help heft the woman. No one knows her true name. They call her Namu. She's dropped eight times, but with their assistance we get her to the street.

There's not even half the room needed for her in back, but she's wedged in somehow, this nameless one. The children must sit atop her now, riding like cowpokes.

Sister Lucy kept thieves at bay for a spell, but a sneak thief smashed in the front window while their crew distracted. The fountain has drenched the seats and dash. The radio is gone. As are my cigs and copy of The Coast of Chicago—and far worse, my petty stash from the glove compartment. The smidgeon of monkey repellant I'll need to make it through the day.

"Will you come with us?" I ask the nun.

"Still much to do here." Sister Lucy scribbles on a page and rips it from her Bible.

"Scripture won't help us now."

"Only paper. My friend hangs meat at McCallum's. Out where the stockyards used to be. It's black market, so make sure they know you come from me."

"Guess that's a plan."

"A good one. I'll gather the old and infirm from over there," she says, pointing to a derelict building that would make Cabrini wince.

"I'll be back. When I can. If I can."

I am strangely compelled to tell her my real name instead of the Rawlson ruse and give her Rahman's number, asking a favor—if one or both of them could pay a visit to the Reinhold to check on Winnie … The way I speak of her, Lucy seems to think she's a nine-year-old girl. I do nothing to change her mind.

Out on the western outskirts, I stop to check the map against Lucy's scribbles. In the back, the dead have their final say. Expulsion of infernal vapor from orifices. First the Nicaraguan man, then his mate, then the man again. Back and forth, sounding like a string of words, some last whispered conversation. The mother thinks *We know now— we know*, was said. The daughter heard *She shows how—in shadows— the toll, the truth*. Reading meaning into death farts—that is what the heat has done to us. But it is an unknowable ill wind, and I pretend I didn't hear Ruby saying, *See you soon, Buddha-Kahn*.

Despite AC barely keeping a livable eighty-eight degrees inside the wagon, I crack windows to expel the unbearable stench, and heat seizes all within. Those who do not throw up, faint.

Up ahead, a cinderblock structure glows in the dying light of sunset, painted gorgeous from the palette of a hundred fires. Nothing marked on any walls, until I park and walk near enough to find scrawled just above the nipple of a buzzer: *This is McCallum's. You better know us. If you don't, you still have time to run.*

I laugh reading it. How could I not? A camera watches, and I nod its way, brace myself and breathe deep. Heavy footsteps approach inside, then there's a rattle of locks and a door swings wide as sweet winter rolls out. A stout old man with an unlit cigar sniffs me over.

"Sister Lucy sent us."

He makes sure I see the handle of his belt-tucked gun.

"Mercy. That's all I got," I tell him.

The man looks out at the ambulance packed to the gills.

"Tough times, I guess. Okay."

I drive in under a roll-top metal gate, which drops back down as soon as I pass. Swaying carcasses everywhere, and red-smeared butcher-paper packages stacked high. My flesh, on the verge of collapse all week, is cured of every cellular ill within minutes. As lush a welcome as any fix.

The Zoroastrians make a nest in the corner. Huddle and pray.

"All Gods are one tonight. May they listen for once."

Miss Alabam lies in the soiled truck, nursing another oxygen tank empty. All will help wash and carry her before I head back out into the night.

The stout man assists me with the perished ones. Together we wrap them several times in plastic, then build an igloo of ice around them.

"Names?" asks the stout man.

"Marie and Jesus."

"Serious?"

"What I heard. Gonna be a lot of dying without knowing exactly who."

"Lucy sent you? She all right?"

"Right in her wheelhouse. Made for such times," I tell him, sharing a look of deep admiration.

"We were common law seven years till she took up the cloth again. Lucky to have those, being an unrepentant sinner and all. We ran a nightclub for Momo, if you can believe that. Twelve years older'n me. Lapsed nun she was then. Then got herself unlapsed. The things she's seen. Calcutta—those favelas down there in Brazil. A year in the heat vents of Ulaanbaatar with feral kids. God knows how many other hellholes."

"She knew your worth, man. Sent us here with faith in you."

I put an arm around him as he breaks down. A festival of tears and quaking. "May I bring more of the lost and stricken?" He laughs and waves his hands in a gesture I take for consent.

## THE NIGHT CANNOT BREATHE ANOTHER BREATH

Most of the county grid shuts down after five more loads are brought back to the meat locker. It will stay cool in the blackness two more days despite the little campfire the stout man keeps going in the corner of his office. Every block of ice I load going out melts in minutes. Not until I leave for the last time do I notice the faded signage on another condemned building on the lot—Gillespie & Gillespie Meat Company.

The last trip to Cicero, the vehicle is only half filled, and for once, no other criticals are waiting. I come upon an incongruous sight: six humbled gang members of rival colors, all too weak to stand, being IV'd by Lucy and Rahman. Both of them say I look like I'm about to drop.

"Not till the temperature does. Back in a jiffy."

"What is this jiffy?" Rahman asks Lucy.

"You know—three shakes of a dead lamb's tail," Lucy says to stump him with more quaint Americana.

After staring a long confused moment, Rahman breaks out in gut-bust laughter. We all do, the gang kids too. At nothing. Because at this moment we all need it as much as oxygen. When ribs have ceased throbbing and our faces melt from the rictus of involuntary grinning, I try to convince them that Winnie's AC might be just the saving grace for those in the ambulance and any more we might yet find. I tell them the electricity at McCallum's, like two-thirds of the city, is on the blink now.

They won't let me leave on my own to go check up on things at the Reinhold Arms. Both squeeze in front. I will not let Rahman drive.

"This is all on me," I insist. "You were never here, okay?"

The chariot slinks sans flash and siren all the way to Windsomer, an echo of all the other times haunting me as we pull up for the last one and park where the flowers have died.

Lucy and Rahman begin to comb the lower floors, seeking more of the overcome, as I hike up through the dark stairwell. Extra batteries in my pocket, a webbing sling if needed to haul down Winnie's brittle bones. The air is oppressive, like water on the bottom of the sea at some ungodly pressure per square inch.

The junkie door stands open. A knowing stench and silence. They are gone, one way or another, all of them. My demon half wants to pillage every inch inside for some portion of a discarded gram. I am dope sick, in early stage heat prostration and on the verge of diabetic coma. Left foot inches inward—but my weight and better angels pull me back with the right one. Something smolders in the kitchen, then fire erupts in full as I pull the door tight.

Let it all fucking burn!

My Halligan tool jacks the door from its hinges, and light sweeps through Winnie Gillespie's suite. The place is vast and dark, mist hugging the floor, a chill intact as back-up diesel generators pump out a cool forty-six degrees. I call out and am unanswered. Decades of dust swaddles every cluttered object. What appears to be silver bullion is stacked ten feet high and tarnished to a dull filthy hue. Robbie Temple's Crestomobile is there, dismantled and reassembled seven stories up. The deepest red I've ever seen. Hundreds, maybe thousands of slide rules in a wanton pile like Pick-Up Sticks.

I approach a tiny portrait in a gilded frame. Young Winnie in a pink dress. Stylized and heroic, doll in hand—faceless human forms elongated in the chiaroscuro darkness behind her. I cannot stop staring at this perfect child. As I reach out to touch it, a voice calls—and I turn. *Buddha-Kahn!* Only Ruby ever called me that.

Tattoos writhe on someone who appears before me. Ribbie and Roobarb—defunct Comiskey Park mascots who never quite caught on. In the midst of a lewd act. These are her tats, but this is not my dead love—just some glowing alabaster thing with obsidian eyes, playing cards with a little girl. All dealt from a tarot deck, each one the ten of swords. They smile my way and wave for me to join them.

"We need a third for Hearts," they chime in unison.

I have begun to slowly dissolve—out of Chicago and into this room. I want to join the game, I want to sleep forever in the cool bliss here, but tell them a better game is underway and they should follow me down to the street.

"You can play in the hydrant with a water sprite!" I promise them.

The slide rule in one wraith's hand flashes into a syringe, and she is a fully cackling Ruby now. Little Winnie's eyes reflect a roaring fire, but she smiles and the flames are extinguished. She stands, and with each step she takes across the dusted floor to the wall where the portrait hangs, she grows and ages, all the while her face skewered by a sliver of light across it, as if struck by a ray through a barely opened door. She tells me how a young Thomas Benton Hart was commissioned to paint her during his two-year stint at the Art Institute of Chicago. After they bought the paper and fired Franklin Meeks, the Gillespie family paid for the portrait to be published on a full page every year on her birthday. Great sums were spent to procure every last copy of the infamous sketch of the privileged brat who skipped upon skulls to safety in the theater fire. Hundred-year-old Winnie pulls the last existing one from a pocket on the back of the frame. She unfolds the brittle pulp, which crumbles to dust in her hand, then hands me the painting and the few remaining cloth remnants of Sabatha, her ancient Bru doll.

"For my only friend."

I slip both items into the folds of the webbing sling. Smoke begins to fill the room, fighting the mist for obfuscation, as voices call my name from down the bile-green hall. The familiar squeak of gurney wheels.

Knees buckle, and the floor rises to meet my face.

My parents had come to visit while I was comatose. They'd left my favorite home-cooked foods, a simple card they bought in the gift shop along with a Buddy Bear. But they did not stay until I woke. Perhaps hoped I never would—the concrete truth in front of them worse than all the dark possibility I'd made them endure during the incommunicado years. A junkie EMT. Their benign imaginations had me happy somewhere, no doubt, a struggling creative sort; a convert to some religious cult at worst.

Rahman had met them and declared I was indeed a fine young man doing noble work. He defended me—as a son. Astonished they were not proud. Furious they would leave before I woke. He'd smiled oddly telling me all this—a twinkle in his eye. A concealment. I would not find out for two more years, when I came down off the mountain and returned for a visit, that he nearly left his family for Lucy and she nearly left the church again. They counsel immigrants and the aged together in Cicero, where Lucy grew up, the great-grandniece of one Alphonse Capone. Both kept their vows in the end. What bond they have is more than enough to satisfy what they need from one another. Rather than the disdain I'd feared, Rahman feels the divine at work with the Khan/Kahn connection. What more he told me, I refused to believe.

Winnie Gillespie died seven weeks before the heat wave.

## HOMEWOOD

I was late to the service on the outer edge of the metropolis. I came to pay something—respect, more penance. Not for Winnie (who indeed had been buried in the family plot in Sheboygan), but for three hundred unclaimed souls laid out in serpentine trenches of worm-wriggling loam. Caskets like runes strewn or the spine of some plesiosaur. Cheap boxes of repurposed wood and cement nails.

Is this Rwanda? Kosovo or Cambodia? The shame! People choose Chicago because there is a machine here that gets things done. Snow falls and is salted away while you dream or an alderman gets the boot. A hard, simple town. But fair, always fair. Not this time.

The dead here outlived everyone they knew, or were abandoned by them. More than half are nameless. Left this Earth with not a single other soul in their lives. The wind stops to remember. Even leaves are moved to silence. Though the heat has crested, it's still balmy and uncomfortable. Shirtless youths begin to toss dirt on top of the coffins, echoing a dull thud down the line. Heavy machinery grinds on, standing by to fill the ground whole.

I watch a scrawny, spotted boxer weave downline, following its snout in search of its perished owner. Panting heavily, slobber dribbling in great foaming gobs, it was miles from wherever home had been, growling at anyone who would halt its mission. The dog finds a particular casket near me and sniffs in circles, building from a low moan to a high-pitched howl filled with such sorrow that all work halts a moment. The old dog paws at the wood, whimpering, digging furiously, then finally, in acceptance or exhaustion, curls up on it.

The Reaper isn't any fearsome wraith; death is only slow, relentless attrition, a breaking down on the cellular level and the civic. Atrophy of oxygen, of compassion, of companionship. In the aftermath, as everyone threw blame like monkeys with their excrement, I was an easy target—the rogue healer gone off the reservation. *Rawlson lied about his name and other pertinent facts, broke protocol, turned his radio off. Illegally borrowed and did not return the vehicle to the motor pool. Ralston used supplies unauthorized and perhaps OD'd on some of them.*

A plain-dressed minister walks down the line. He's presided over the unclaimed souls of Cook County for years now. Homewood is his charge, and the flow of the forgotten is a constant sorrow. He wishes the world could know that. The anomalous heat wave made headlines, but this happens every single fucking day in every single fucking town of any size.

The aberration brought a brief light to bear on the plight of those who outlive their people. A tiny clot of media came to newsbyte the sadness of it all, the harsh truth that almost no one showed to mourn these dead. My photo was taken—head hanging, tears streaming, still in my CC EMS windbreaker, bringing that dog a bowl of water. I became a minor iconic figure for a week or two. The overworked Joe who cared. My own "fifteen minutes"—for empathy, not infamy. The Department hated me even more for that. Rahman sent copies out to Barstow.

I left Illinois with a single duffle bag and the pooch who mourned an unknown friend.

## LICKING WOUNDS ON THE ROOF OF THE WORLD

I've gone as far away from that Chicago summer as I possibly could. In centigrade and longitude, in attitude and altitude. I supervise a clinic in Nepal during spring and summer with a couple Gurkahs and their wives. I'm the doctor when the doctor is not here, which is often. The rest of the year I live humbly in Lumbini and help other volunteers rebuild the waterworks. The vague plan is to stay here till I turn twenty-nine, then walk down and join the world again. Worked okay for Gautama.

Winnie left most of her holdings to the U of Chi and other charities, but some were parceled out to staff and distant relatives. And an undeserved portion came to me. I set up a scholarship at SOM in Fazlur's name. Paid my parents' mortgage off and other such gifting.

I live penniless as possible in a cinderblock abode with a wood-burning stove, the boxer, now named Homewood ("Homey"), always at my hip. That Thomas Hart Benton is the only treasure I possess. A tiny rouge island on the ocean-gray wall—exactly opposite a small window with a universe-class view of Kanchenjunga. Storm clouds roiling endlessly across the Himalayas. They are significant entities up here, the breath of Gods. I have order and simplicity. The needs of others keep me distracted from my own. I sleep well from good exhaustion. In dreams, though, I am haunted still by lust, chaos, and regret.

Time to time I'll read from some dog-eared paperback I brought (Stuart Dybek stories mostly) and wonder what's the what back in the Second City. Ponder deep dish and Ditka, all that's good about the humble berg. And every useless jagoff I ever met as well. Part of my soul will always be there. A portion still at Princeton and in Baltimore, and way too much left back in County Kern. My dream now is to be of some new place, become another me with better memories, looking back on a life yet to be lived.

On occasion, I stoke a fire with extra fuel, boil water to steam the room, bundling up in layers of fleece till a lather of sweat (and a small chew of the local *wolsbane*) brings back the veil of madness. *Some cleansing ritual, if you will.* Every once in a while, I'm sure Ruby can be glimpsed in the serpentine shadows behind Winnie in the portrait. That *why not?* smile. Flames crackle, and I hear her tender, wicked laugh beckon once more.

Two daughters of privilege—one who embraced oblivion in league with another who lived long beyond a destined fate. It all stirs a maelstrom within me. Sometimes Robbie Temple calms things with a song.

Is this a bit of true magic, conjured by ordeal, artistry, and al-chemy into century-old paint somehow? Or only the trick of thin air, heat, and my synapses dying—one—by—one?

# EXIT LEFT

The cold metal doors slam shut, and I am sealed in, coffin-like, for a smattering of seconds or even, dear God, a minute or more. But this will pass. I will endure; I always have.

Breathe now—slow, from the gut, deep down within the solar plexus. Slower—till the lungs, every inch, are full and aching. Hold as long as you can.... Exhale.

Better. Darkness is receding. Yes. I control this space. I control my fate. Breath of life, breath of life, breath of life.

*DING!* My eyes open with the elevator doors, and I move to exit this vertical casket, but a short, corpulent woman with the name tag "Diz" smiles at me and blocks my path.

"Wrong floor, sweetheart; think you want seven," she says. Indeed, my floor button is still illuminated. Doors and darkness close in again, and we ride in silence.

Diz senses my plight, relinquishing as much elevator space as she can. She could never know, however, that I have very good reason to be phobic of small spaces. After all, in my early youth I had once been trapped in a smashed-up Buick, submerged in a river bottom with my family dead all around me. Two tons of Detroit steel plummeting down through algae. Father and Mother floating as if in space—foreheads stove in. The windshield spider-cracked, blood swirling like galaxies in the water from the glow of the flashlights approaching. I survived off trapped air from an empty thermos till those divers came.

Well, actually—no, that's not really true. That was just a story I told Carol to work her emotions, wasn't it? It had happened to my friend Kurt, not me. I told her a great many such tales, until I believed them all to be true. And not just her, but Fran, and Winnie, Celeste, and the others. My invented past can seem so real. God knows I utilize it every chance imaginable for "sense memory." Pathetic, isn't it, to have no real trauma of your own? Is it my fault my upbringing as the only child of diplomats was so nurturing and uneventful? I've always been jealous of those raw-nerve actors with some hellish past to draw upon. Such grist for the creative mill. Maybe that's why I am still a nobody with an ever-closing five-year window to play leads. And am rapidly losing my hair. And perhaps my mind. Why else would I try to stir up faux claustrophobia to cover the anticipatory dread of an audition? And for a television part, no less?

I peek at Diz. She's on her way back from the Xerox, a fresh set of "sides" in her hands. She holds their warmth up to her face, sniffs the sweet chemical reek wafting off them, relishing it. Odd.

The elevator doors open, and I, the handsomish everyman—early thirties to mid-forties—Josh Barnes, exhale into the casting anteroom. A dozen others, all from the same narrow band of eerily similar likeness, are spaced around the room. Some I know; some I know too well. Most sit. Many pace—like fish in a tank, all giving each other as wide a berth as they possibly can. Everyone has the same three pages stapled at the corner. The room silent but for rustling paper and the compound murmuring.

I endure forty-five minutes of such hell, then a voice calls from across the room. I keep my breathing steady and take measured steps over to a card-table setup.

"You're here for the lead, right?" says Diz.

What? Is she kidding? I'm not right for the lead? This lead? Any lead? Was that an insinuation? Who is she to judge me, this chubby muffin, this failed commercial actress wannabe.

"Course you are, cute-stuff. Just the first two scenes, and we are ten behind at least, so it's gonna be short and sweet. Like me." She winks, then leads me into . . . The Room.

It is beige on beige, dim, and far too large for this activity. A harsh spotlight on a C stand roasts a high-back wooden chair. A video camera beams a steady red dot.

Three figures sit at a long table with notebooks and refreshments in front of them. I am led to this tribunal that will mete out judgment upon my soul. Or at least my career.

"This is Josh Barnes, a multi-Obie-nominated vet of local theater. He's done all the Dick Wolf shows too," Diz says, then leaves, her heels echoing into the hall.

The unholy Trinity consists of: Ian, the director, who is pale as a corpse (with about the same pleasant demeanor), long unkempt hair, and hideously expensive pre-distressed leather jacket; Saul, the producer, who sports a supernatural tan and dazzling teeth that can't be real; and, lastly, the casting director, Marla, a woman wearing so many layers upon layers of billowy fabric, with masses of orange-brown locks and huge tinted glasses obscuring her heavily made-up face, one can only guess what she really might look like underneath it all.

First comes the requisite ritual known as *icebreaking*, a sussing out through unplanned chitchat to obtain a general indication of social comfort level. This is going on a bit longer than usual. Which is good, very good. Someone who has borrowed my skin and my voice is nimbly carrying on in a marvelous urbane style, bantering with these three like we've all known each other since university. Then, with a clearing-of-the-throat signal, it begins: The Audition.

"We're doin' a cop show loosely based on *Hamlet*. Well, inspired by, really," Marla says.

"Rosencrantz and Guildenstern are deadbeats, perhaps?" I quip.

"Pimps, actually," says Saul, trampling my witticism.

"I have, of course, done the Bard on several occasions." I shrug modestly, yet confidently. "*Midsummer* at the Guthrie, three splendid Ashland summers, and twice—in the park—back in the glory of the Papp years. Never the—uh—Scottish play, however, and never shall I."

The director, Ian, loosens into the barest of smiles.

"West End ever?" he says, covering his Midlands accent well, not even bothering to look up from a thorough perusing of my res. A nervous cough scoots out of my mouth before the next train of words leaves.

"Well, hmm, it says something there, I believe—" I say. Or try to. My God, I am nearly stammering, ears pinking, eyes welling with salty tears, a tremor building in my fingers and spreading up my arm.

"Despite my agent's enthusiasm, only as an understudy, I confess," I confess.

Ian looks up, his cold reptilian heart clearly revealed through his narrow gray eyes.

"Well, I saw that particular production," Ian says, then milks a dramatic pause far too long. "Just as well you never made the stage. Truly dreadful." Ian makes a perfect steeple from his bony fingers, resting his semi-cleft chin at the pinnacle. "This, as you may know, is a cutting-edge premium cable television series about an actor of immense talent and meager success who moonlights as a beat cop."

"Versa visa, really," says Saul.

"Pardon?" Ian flinches at this interjection.

Saul sighs, like he has to explain fractions to a child. "Our guy—day job, he's on the job—moonlightin' as a workin' actor. You had it ass backward."

"Saul, I know what moonlighting is. Do you really think I don't?"

Saul shrugs. Ian bristles. And I thank God for someone else's tension filling the room.

"Anyhoo, we are thinking of goin' unknown," Marla says with a wink, meaning this might be the most important day of my entire life.

"Clooney wanted that part in *Sideways*, ya know that? But the director said, nope, I want fresh faces, no star baggage and all that fuckin' crap. Smart kid, that director," Saul says. A none-too-subtle jibe tossed Ian's way.

"He wasn't completely unknown. He'd done a great many things," says Ian.

"Not him—that's the nebbish. I'm talkin' 'bout the other guy—hangdog Nicholson face, bedroom voice." Saul waves his fat-fingered paws, trying to pull the name down from the ether.

"From *Wings*," says Marla.

"Yes! Church. Aiden Timothy Church is his name," states Ian emphatically (and quite wrongly), then throws a look at Saul. "If you keep undercutting my thoughts, I swear..."

"Boys, please!" Marla says. "Let's get on with it." She turns her focus back to me.

"What they are trying to say, Joshua, is that what *Sopranos* did for the then unknown Jimmy Gandolfini, this will do for whosoever we cast. That kinda zeitgeist part. Cable is like that now."

My agent was right. Never was I more perfect for a role. Josh, I tell myself, you have waited a lifetime for this one, and the wait was worth it. Zeitgeist indeed.

The room chills hostile again, simply from Marla asking me to *Read, please*. Cold read. A trained chimpanzee, am I? To dance for your pleasure and ridicule? Were we not fast friends just a moment ago? Now a test is suddenly required? A lifetime's work to be distilled and displayed in an inadequate, haphazard snippet with no relevance whatsoever to theater, cinema, or even cable acting.

Nevertheless, I courageously barrel through the shopworn Shakespeare chestnuts condensed and truncated in the sides for the read. But I do the actual text from memory, which seems to please Ian but thoroughly confuse Saul. Then, finally, I am requiered to utter some truly awful modern law-enforcement dialogue.

"Freeze, you piece-of-shit skell! Come out now and live a decent life. Or stay in that would-be tomb and die a miserable, forgotten death!" I say without believing a word of it.

And it's over. I can feel it. A dead-air pause hanging in the room like fresh gun smoke. Saul pours another glass of water. Marla checks her watch, stifling a yawn. Well, I admit that last part fell somewhere on the lackluster spectrum. Perhaps I should ask to give it a second go? And what exactly is a skell? Skeleton? Oh yes, of course! I should have used a Yorick reference. Should have done something—anything other than that bland, atrocious read.

I sigh, ready to stand and walk out of the room to my empty existence. Back to scraping by to keep up monthlies on three maxed credit cards. Back to the prospect of dinner theater in the Poconos or a cruise performance of *Cactus Flower*. Back to a long, slow suicide disguised as a life.

"Now that we've done the basic shtick, I'd like to venture off book, so to speak, and do a little exercise," Ian says. Saul rolls his eyes and makes a "jerking-off" hand motion, mouthing Ian's words silently to himself.

Ian makes me repeat those same trite lines again and again, each time with a new patois or brogue that he tosses to me at the last possible instant.

"South Boston! Appalachian. Irish! Cockney. French! Aussie. Jamaican! Mentally challenged! Afrikaner!" shouts Ian. This is all a perfect showcase for my talents. Thank God for Gary Austin's improv workshop those eight years in the valley. And Easton's dialect classes, worth every penny, more than Northwestern and Juilliard combined. Not only do I bat back each volley with near flawless diction and tasteful nuance, I even assume radical new postures to complement each voice. The loping gait of a tall Jamaican. The impudent squat of a small Frenchman. The bodily blarney of an inebriated Celt. The casting director can't help smiling. The producer nods approval to her. But this coy director covers his face, trying to hide what must be his pleasure with my seasoned, protean craft. Finally, he stares for a long moment.

"Yes, very nice indeed, Mr. Barnes," Ian says, then milks another interminable pause. "But can you be—street? Our character has a certain, well, lower socioeconomic background. You seem a bit well-fed, well-bred."

"We may go ethnic," says Marla.

"Depends on the talent pool out there," Saul says.

"You have a well-trained instrument, but the question here is one of believability. *Street cred,* as they say." Ian is laying down a new gauntlet for me.

I am hiding behind a weakening grin, then it dawns on me—Josh, you must simply channel one Eddie Pelotti, the worst roommate who ever lived. Use him, embody him. Let his animalistic fervor, even his bad cologne, fill the room. Why hadn't I done that for the skell line? Had I used him for that, there would be no street cred question.

"Mr. Barnes, I know it's a lot to ask, but could you take a stab at that street thing for us?" Marla says.

I laugh, shake my head with a secret knowledge they can never hope to fathom. I crouch on my haunches in the corner, exhale a fifteen second moan, tapping my primal scream, then slowly boil up to a Joe Pescian anger, moving catlike toward the director.

"Kiddin' me with this shit? You want street, huh? Street? You arrogant little limey cocksucker. You think you can come o'er to my country, my city, my NEIGHBORHOOD, and fuckin' talk like that to me? To ME? I will bitch-slap you back to Birmingham, suck out your eyeballs one by one, and skull fuck you six ways from Sunday! Cuz, not fer nuthin' motherfucker, I AM THESE STREETS!" I boast with a harrowing Red Hook authenticity, charging into the table. Ian jumps back in his chair as if yanked by a rope. I stare a moment too long.

"Scene," I intone and nearly curtsey. Ian exhales with relief. (Thank you, Eddie—I owe you a prime rib dinner should ever our paths cross again, though I believe you still owe me $1,237.43).

"Need to change shorts, Ian?" says Saul, and Ian smiles back. These two adversaries, now united by their adoration of my work. I do a sharp nod and turn to leave, hearing the murmur of what they surely must be whispering to each other now.

"That Barnes ain't half bad," Saul would be saying. "I'm Brooklyn born, so I know, and the kid came close."

"Jimmy G. all over again, swear to God," Marla might say.

"Much potential, indeed," Ian offers. "Well-schooled, his father was Ambassador to Sweden. And takes direction well."

It is a mere dozen steps to the door. Well, actually, there are two doors, but I do not notice this in the least, as I am walking on air, wondering how will I deal with the paparazzi hounding me now that Barnes-mania is on the verge of exploding like a supernova. Zeitgeist! You must remember all this for late-night talk show gab, I tell myself, laughing inwardly as I leave the room—then darkness suddenly closes in once more. What? Why is it dark? A BLACKOUT? Has the power gone off in this twenty-story building? God! All over the city? What's happened?

Then the realization shudders me: instead of exiting back out into the anteroom, I HAVE WALKED INTO A CLOSET. This is where I am. Easy enough to do. Easy enough to undo ... if I immediately laugh and scoot back out—"Whoops, wrong door!"—but I haven't done that. I've waited too long. A moment. A long, awkward one. Too late to come out now, too late! Why am I frozen? I reach out to grip the knob but cannot make my hand begin to twist it. Every second I remain compounds the predicament tenfold.

If I just come out, pulling up my zipper, joking that I went to the men's room or make some feeble "out of the closet" bon mot. Crass humor, but still forgivable.

Perhaps they don't even know what's in this room. Maybe they know nothing about it except that I went in it. That I am in it. A Nixonian sweat begins to soak through every layer of fabric I wear. I must wait this out now, however long it takes. That's all this is—a new burden to bear.

Diz brings in the next actor, a Glen Baltimore. He bested me for a soap two years ago and for Biff in *Salesman* at The Kaleidoscope. What an insipid moniker; my God, he's from Knob Lick, Missouri, the fraud! They begin his icebreaker routine.

My eyes begin to adjust to the dark. I can see there is supply shelving in here but not much more. I gently remove the pencils and pens from a tall cardboard cylinder, fill it to the brim with my bladder's release. Then it starts—the shouting. I nearly drop the container.

"Freeze, you piece-of-shit skell. Come out now!" I know these lines. Lines I've just spoken, but the performance is so forceful, so real, I begin to believe they are meant for me, here in the closet. I am putty in the hands of truthful acting. Yes, I am—just a skell—that is what I am! A piece-of-shit skeleton unworthy of skin. I nearly come out as ordered.

Oh, God, what to do? Why can't I move? I could tell them I wanted this part so badly, I went into the closet on purpose just to recon my competition. Ethically questionable, yes, but admired by them, perhaps—that kind of criminal dedication. Better than the horrible truth that I simply blundered in and was too much of a coward to correct the gaffe.

I crack the door the slightest bit and peek out as Diz brings in the next actor. Her double take leads me to the suspicion that she may have become aware of my situation. If so, I pray she keeps this secret to herself. They cannot know. They can never know.

Actor after actor enters, chits, then chats, spouts Shakespeare, shouts "skell," then leaves. Seconds, minutes, perhaps hours melt into a temporal smear. I rub my eyes, and the phosphenes glow spectral and drift, personifying bright flickerings of my past that float up like carbonated bubbles. Memories, lies, reviews, delusions, soliloquies, fears, footlight glimpses, snapshots of relationships half-forgotten. This is where it all has led you, Josh—on the brink of dreams, yet instead entombed here in abject mortification.

Time to face your harshest truths now, Joshua, starting with the fact your name isn't Joshua or Barnes. It's Oswald Specker. From Fort Logan, North Dakota. You were a sorry, quiet orphan, never the only child of diplomats. Foster charge of a series of lowlife scoundrels and meth-addled mothers. You never set foot in Juilliard. Dropped out of that JC near Northwestern, where you haunted their theater bars, pestering ingénues, wishing to be of their world. Later, marginally, you were. Learning to be a fine chameleon. Regurgitating authors' lines, aping others' lives, feigning and pretending. Your life, O. Speck, has been nothing but one long deceit within a sorry fraud wrapped around a never-ending charade—a chain of interlocking failures, small and great, all competing for the title of weakest link.

The words outside have turned to ocean, a rising and falling surf. My clothes are peeling off in soggy strips, or is it skin? Bile on the verge of leaking out my pores. Joints have seized, locking permanently. I feel as if I have taken my last step in this life. It is madness where I am now.

Whoever you are—do something or disappear forever. At least choose to disappear. Yes! That's a thought. If I could only stop breathing, refuse to take any more of what is autonomically ruled—slow my heart to a stop and still my blood. Yes, that would be something if I could. A true breaking down from the shame of it all into spontaneous human emulsification, like a salted slug. What a righteous act that would be! To will my will to cease.

In the midst of this dark desire something happens. The wish manifests—a soft click rippling through the universe, nothing more. I let go of it all: fear, hope, regret, anger, lust, wealth, family, fame, everything. I slink fetal to the floor. Acceptance renders sweet re-lease, and I disengage from all concerns of the living.

I am rising now, up from darkness, toward infinite light. Drifting through walls, hovering angelic above the mortal fray. Nothing I ever thought mattered really does. Silly thoughts, silly career, silly life. I laugh, as all I once was lies in decay, melting far below me now. I want wings—and I have them. I wish to glide through the great Crab Nebula—and instantly—I do.

In that dim beige room back on dim beige Earth, Saul turns back to the others as they head out the casting room door on their way to lunch.

"This place I'm takin' us has the best puffer fish chef in the states. I dare you to take a bite, Sir Ian, one bite!" says Saul.

"You really are trying to kill me, aren't you?" Ian laughs. "And FYI, I've had fugu at Tokyo many, many times."

A moment later Diz tiptoes near, knocks gently on the closet door.

"You take a nap in there, sweetie?" she whispers, pulling the door open, then dropping down to examine the quivering, melted shape on the floor—clothes dissolved in protoplasm, still steaming from the cellular breakdown. The viscous mass burns her hand when she touches it, a heavenly acid stinging her with joy. Tears flow as she raises her hand to behold the glowing halo around it.

"Tough little sitch ya got yourself into, huh, babe? I'll never tell—trust the Diz on this."

I let her words ensnare me, and suddenly I begin to fly backward, down from the Crab Nebula, hurtling through a wormhole in the Milky Way—descending back toward Terra and inflating my sorry flesh again.

"You got it. You and two others. Callback. Thursday."

"Zeitgeist," I hear myself whisper as the sound of her heels slowly fades.

# HARMONY ARM

What Earl Gunderson could have now is what he's never sought—a great sum of money and not a goddamn thing to do.

To make it through another year and not lose everything he put into the ground was always enough in payment. To will seeds to sprout and watch them writhe toward the sun just as he and God had planned was enough purpose—but Earl has little choice now but to lie fallow or go till himself a grave and hope to harvest a better, everlasting life on the other side of this one.

"Take the check or fight ten years in court. These bastards own 'em and Congress too," says Chester Fulton, a one-time acquaintance, now the fat mouthpiece mediating on behalf of corporate bandits trying to steal Earl's family land. "Go spree with all that green somewheres. What me and any hundred men'd do. Women—what have you."

Chester can see the what-have-you appeal stick in Earl's craw as they share an awkward reptilian glance. The last time they'd seen each other, right here in this barn, was half their lives ago. A day Earl has banished and buried deep.

"How much time you got with all that eatin' you up inside? They'll just wait you out."

Sauget-Prochem Industries knows more about Earl than he's forgotten about himself. Any haywire thing he's ever said demanding the floor down at the Grange Hall; every dime of loan, sale, and tax; the full prognosis of Earl's malignancy. Why do they even want the worthless dirt his kin staked back when Van Buren was president? More sand than soil, and so bereft of nutrients no native nation ever claimed it. Bad water. Bad spirits. Yet Gundersons took it on and made it give up sustenance. Chester tells him SPI wants it because it *is* subpar shit-soil, a fine analogue for the third world. Where all the future growth will be. So take it as a blessing.

"Wanna sit down face to face with the one what done this," Earl tells him. "Look them in the eyes and let 'em tell me why."

"It was a corporate decision, Earl. Ain't no *them* to see. Somebody made an assessment, and the board ruled on it."

"Then it can be unruled back again."

Chester relights a stogie near chubby as he is and takes a draw. Ash falls and sets some straw aglow. Earl steps quick to stamp it out.

"Train's long gone, and there's no more track. Nothin' I can do."

How does one look in the eyes of such a Medusa snakefest of them, Earl ponders. A body that, if the head is severed, will just grow another. SPI were well-known death merchants under a different moniker, Mawr-Sauget Allied Poison. They made fine elixirs sure to kill the most cantankerous of pests. (Gundersons had used them on weed and varmint for decades.) But with a locust greed, they'd expanded their enterprise a hundredfold the last few years, gobbling up every other seed outfit, toying with the strains in unholy ways, and now seem hell-bent to own the very nature of food itself.

They bought the Culbertson spread to Earl's west, the Hinshaws' ten thousand to the east, the McWhorters' and Sathes' too, and made test farms of them. Grew their demon corn and devil wheat. The capricious wind wafted kernels all the way to the Gunderson furrows to take root and elbow out Earl's alfalfa with genetic black magic. His aquifer, tainted with a lethal brew of pesticidal runoff, was useless now, and the probable blame for his tumored flesh and lack of platelets. They have him under siege. Earl is the only holdout in the county—the last Gunderson to toil upon this land.

A "fair offer" has been made—generations of sweat and peril quantified into a six-figure sum. They'll allow Earl three days of mulling.

The world has done its level best to run his family from these acres before, and every time the world has failed. Drought and flood, anthrax and hoof-and-mouth, diphtheria and influenza. On top of those—the depressions of 1850, 1902, and of course The Great One. Anytime he's ever felt sorry for himself, thinking his times were hard, Earl would thank his enormous fortune to be born into the life he was, and give nod to the *wirral blod* he comes from, Vikings upon a time, ones to never give up—and if pushed to fight, a people who avenge.

Had John Belushi lived—gone moon-bald, his skin roasted cancerous in summer and spider-cracked blue in winter; if he'd been 6'4" and lost half his choppers too—he might look much like Earl does today. The barrel chest. The wild-hare eyes. Dexterous eyebrows and a seldom given, dangerous grin. But Earl, a man who does not peruse mirrors and has never owned a television, would not know this. He's read his Greek and Roman myths. The entire Frank Baum oeuvre. Sundry other tomes his kin and common-law mate had left behind. Earl knows what he knows, and it's been enough, but the whole of the frenzied world out there is of another tongue to him, and he cannot fathom the appeal of much of it. Where could he possibly go now that could ever be called home?

For two days Earl walks his land, row by row, remembering. He makes a point of touching every fence post tamped down in the hardpan by one dead Gunderson or another. Each scar and healed fracture. Sacred spots of buried hounds and other animals worth naming. The resting place of Edith. What will become of the family plot along a creek gone dry back before the moon landing? Earl's not seen a gopher in a decade, nor a firefly. When the seventeen-year-cicada plague filled the eastern seaboard skies a few years ago, Earl barely saw a dozen here. Like a solemn Penelope, he waits for the bees to return from wherever they've gone. Nothing would cheer his heart as much as the comforting frizz of a swarm around him again.

Earl hikes up a mini-butte at the hogback of his acreage, yanking on a rope ladder to best the steepest parts. The only parcel that will be left him—this five-acre tabletop with its 360-degree horizon view. His Little Anvil. SPI says he can grow subsistence crops up here if he wishes, letting Earl keep some familial connection to the land. Topsoil long gone and too gusty to ever be a prime field, but he's been hauling his best fallow earth and mulch to the base for weeks, stowing it on the leeward side. There's a little rain catcher of a cavern eroded in the limestone up there. He could build a windbreak and checkerboard a crofting field, grow some tenacious barnacle of a crop.

Fortunate to be prairie born, Earl has been queasy of heights his entire life, and standing here has always wrought knots in his belly till he near blacks out. But this time it feels almost pleasant—the tingling vertigo of a playground swing.

Earl had thought up a theory when he was a youngster still hoping for science as a trade. He figured since we were monkeys in bygone times, that sensation you get on a swing set at the crest of the arc is just nerves down in the solar plexus sending signals to that old tail to reach out and catch a branch, but being's how we've lost them—it just gets all scrambled now without a where to go.

Impressed with Earl's creative thinking, Ma let him in on some oddball Gunderson history. In the nineteenth century, half the clan had briefly given themselves over to an offshoot of the Charles Fourier Phalanx and run off to Utopia, Ohio. This collectivist movement believed that if humans could live together in peace for sixteen generations, a new appendage would evolve, a human tail called a Harmony Arm. It would be as powerful as an alligator's, but supple as a cat's. A sort of prehensile hand flexing at the tip—a huge thumb and two fingerish knobs with the retractable talons of an eagle. This reenvisioned noble ape in touch with his true nature would flourish, wielding the tail-arm as a labor aid, weapon, and even a source of sensual pleasure. Naturally, it was a failure of a dream.

Earl was never sure if Ma was joshing when she claimed that, as testament to those early Gundersons and their stalwart believings, one in three of the extended family had been born with a vestigial piglet tail, some as long as seven inches, still glistening with tawny lanugo. Doc Grandey always snipped them quick, before the newborn's first bawling. Some of the witchy aunts supposedly kept a specimen jar with dozens for use in ancient harvest rituals.

Ma would never say if this was true of him, but young Earl sometimes wished himself a tail so bad he couldn't sleep. He was sure he could feel the scar back there atop his heinie, and scratched his coccyx madly in hopes of making it grow. Of all life's iniquitous fates, to have been robbed of this seemed the worst.

After umpteen Gunderson litters down through the years, each containing nine offspring on average, Earl's folks could baste up but a solitary child. Punished for trying too late in life, perhaps. Fed up with harsh life, the remaining families all moved off the land during the dust bowl, and come Earl's teens, it was down to just his folks and hired hands to work the farm.

It was up here on the anvil where Earl had been orphaned. His thirteenth Fourth of July. The three had finished with their picnic, all set to make the rocket's red glare with eighteen boxes of fireworks from the Rez. They watched a distant storm roll in over the plains. The thunderhead was still miles away, but the air had charged ahead of it, and out of a clear blue sky a great forking bolt roared down from Olympus, igniting black powder, and in an obliterating flash, his parents were fused into sand. Right next to Earl, who hadn't as much as a stitch undone. The arbitrary precision was of some vengeful deity— and Earl, his whole heathen life, would never bow to any group who claimed a Good Lord above. What was left of his folks—bone dust and fulgurite—remains to this day, a glassine lump in the shade of a dwarf chestnut tree.

Earl touches his shrine tenderly. "A child never had no one better," he whispers and kisses it twice, then sidles over to loose earth at the edge of the butte, closes his eyes and, filling his one lung deep, just steps off into thin air. A halfhearted gesture, nothing suicidal, meant only to shake loose the rust of his lessening days. Unlike some cartoon animal's, Earl's feet do not blur in frantic motion and defy gravity. He plummets like an ordinary stone, lands butt-side down and slides most of the way, but the last twenty feet are all a-tumble. A rib cracks loose in there somewhere, and his patella and rotator cuff are badly wrenched, but he makes it to his feet and ambles awkward back toward the farmhouse. For an hour Earl soaks himself in ice, then drives the forty miles to Prairie Heights.

In the last decade, there was a Super Bowl ad pimping the shiny new Dodge Rams. The resonant voice of Paul Harvey, Voice of the Heartland, had been resurrected. A tinny, scratched recording of a bygone era—"So God Made a Farmer"—was set against gold-lit snippets of hard men of the soil. It showcased the leathered cheeks, the pluck and well-earned fatigue—a poem to general goodness on the plains. America had leaked salty tears for the plight of the endangered dirt farmer. For a day, maybe even a week, then promptly forgot. Went back to Applebee's and ate their factory chicken, microwaved more synthetic goo. Umbrage—such a transient thing these days. We know what we should do about so much, but are soon bedazzled by this and enchanted by that, then dissuaded by nonsense until we shirk away. Every damn one of us.

Earl had seen the commercial once down at Morehouse Feed. The young fella trying to run his daddy's enterprise had a magic box that could capture old shows from the television, and he played it just for Earl.

"Hey Gunny—missed your chance—you'da been the perfect old farmer, dude!"

Earl just harrumphed, spat a rainbow of tobacky, and said nobody he knew could afford them shiny new things. Besides, Gundersons were always Ford people; he still drives Old Blue, his '64 Two-Story Falcon.

Earl meets Chester at Lacey's Biscuit, a diner on the outskirts, and over gaucho steak and flannel cakes, he makes his mark on a contract he does not even bother reading—takes the check and stares at it for half an hour, unable to speak. Chester, as per agreement, leaves a giant roll of fifty-dollar bills on the table and a stock certificate, then silently skedaddles.

What has Earl gone and done? Kin rolling in their caskets now. The itch of SPI poison building in his guilty veins. Earl considers signing the check over to Lacey and leaving it for a tip so as to rid himself of the foul taint, but drives farther on down the half-boarded-up main street, passing the ghostly silhouette of the old high school for sale on eBay with a 50k Buy It Now—all the way to 24/7 PayDay Loans, a check-cashing establishment next to the Speedy Mart in a rundown pod mall on the far side of town.

"Sure you wanna do this?" asks the young woman working the counter.

"Bank closed me out after this last rough patch. Got et by a bigger fish, not local no more. Been a Gunderson account with 'em since the Civil War—then it's *Sorry, we don't know you.*"

"Seriously—it's a really big bite we take."

Earl says that will have to do, and most likely he'll not have time to spend the half of it anyways. The girl sees a lot of her own farmer dad in the thousand-yard stare of Earl's deep-set errant eyes and stooping sinew. She arranges a prepay credit card with a monumental amount and shows him how to use it.

"Now you go see Luanne over in Dunbar—second floor of Penny's—back in the Hallmark section. She'll get you on a world cruise somewhere. Maybe those fjords. Back to Sweden—see your people."

Even though that was almost two hundred years ago, and his heritage is Norwegian, Earl thinks about it. Ponders the Grand Canyon, Yosemite and other such postcard staples. He'd love to see an ocean or the glorious tabernacles of baseball stadiums he's only read of in The Sporting News. Are there any original structures left but Wrigley and Fenway? Earl takes some comfort that at least he lived long enough to hear his beloved Cubs finally win the World Series on the radio last summer.

Earl decides on Vegas, closest thing to the Emerald City in this world, he imagines, and nearby two Gundersons who'd gone out to work on Hoover Dam are still buried in the concrete with a hundred others. He's heard it is a true wonder of the world, and surely it must be time for Lady Luck to smile upon him when he tries the myriad games of chance.

After calling around to several hotels, Earl has a revelation and finds his life purpose as if this was all meant to be. Sauget-Prochem Industries will be taking over Vegas for a stockholders meeting next month. With three other smaller conventions the same Fourth of July week, rooms are scarce, but Earl has his Judas sum, and it will buy him a luxury high-roller suite in the main hotel of the SPI event, leaving more to wild-spree with if he should wish. Specificity has not yet formed, just a general compunction to venture there and find a proper fulcrum for the vengeance eating up his soul.

\* \* \*

Earl tosses his medicines away and spends his last month planting up on the butte, paying an extended family of Oaxacan cousins five times their usual to aid him. They turn several outbuildings into three modest abodes and find a heretofore unknown spring. Earl learns to love stewed mole. He wills the deed of his Little Anvil to the Guelatao clan if he should not return, long as they tend the crystalline shrine. In appreciation, two of their bunch go so far as to legally change their names to Humberto and Rufino Gunderson. Their widowed sister, Clementina, goes further, and despite Earl's shy resistance, thanks him carnally. He hopes against the odds that another seed might be left to grow in the world when he's gone. Earl Jr. or Earlina. The Oaxacans promise to grow the heirloom beets Earl's planted in large-rowed patterns spelling out—*F U C K - Y O U - S P I ! !*—for every flyover asshole up there to see.

Earl carefully removes an old wooden case from a locked cabinet in the barn, the name Beaver Brand faded on the label. Earl knows this family outfit out of Bismarck was gobbled up by his nemesis corporation back in the '80s. A honeyed liquid drips from the worm-corroded bottom. It makes Earl cry, to think of honey. He'd long been the best apiarist in the county—king of overwintering queens—and he is sure these same devils that drive him from his land have done them in as well.

It's quiet on the farm this evening without any animal presence. No gentle footsteps padding, no soothing exhalations. Only wind and creaking roof, the soft whisper of shifting soil. Earl considers flinting a flame right here and now and going out with a royal bang. Then his rare, wicked smile grows ear to ear—yes, that would be a thing to do—but not here, and not alone. How poetic the justice will be for those who render death so blithely to have acquired the means of their own demise. A lesson from some myth.

Earl turns the leaking case over every six hours for the next two days, letting the parched sawdust soak back the nitroglycerin bleeding out. He packs things carefully in charcoal wrap, then again in oiled canvas. Makes three separate batches that all fit tightly into standard USPS boxes, addressed to and from Chester Fulton, c/o Caesars Palace.

Deep under the hay, Earl finds a mason jar with what appears to be twenty-seven snipped-off tails, ghostly pale, floating in some pickled concoction. He takes sips from a jar of horrid akvavit moonshine stowed there too, from back in the '20s, his kin trying to cheat the revenue man and supplement the harvest. It renders him blotto in no time as he torches the barn—watching it roast away all night till nothing's left but memories and fading embers. Voices call from the crackle of flame, some telling him he done right, others damning his soul. Two things happened in this barn that should be scorched from the face of earth forever. Earl incinerates all traces of Gunderson possession and history, books and diaries, tintype photographs of old sod homes and county fair trophies. He keeps one fat, flowery first-place ribbon and fixes it to the jar of tails. Other than the Beaver Brand and this, Earl will walk clean and unencumbered into whatever his last brief phase of life shall bring.

After his folks' demise, a Sunday school teacher was sent to be Earl's guardian by a wealthy uncle who'd left and made his mark in sourdough out in San Francisco Bay. The woman lived alone in the bunkhouse, the boy in the main. Thirty-six to his fourteen. She taught him well enough to read magazines and keep books, and she Bible'd him some, though not as much as one would expect. Mainly fables from the good book, Noah's ark and such. Earl resisted anything more.

Such a scandal when she took up under the same roof, never filing proper papers for adoption. The neighbors thought it was conniving at best, or plain unnatural, taking advantage of a simple boy. She and Earl would cavort, pretending they were various creatures—barking, purring, snorting, and nipping at each other. They spooned for warmth, then companionship. At some point, lubricated by a bottle of port from a case his folks had left in the cellar, this led to where it naturally would.

Both balked and shied away once it was done. They barely spoke for weeks, but if one of them left another bottle out, the other soon partook, and the inevitable would follow. They'd be man and woman for a moment, then back to strained silence, then teacher/student again. This silly bitter dance played on another year, till she lost patience and tried to switch midstream from loving support to an iron-rod mode, and he buckled under the new reins, no longer lying with her. The schoolmarm upped the ante, trying to irk a jealous streak by bedding hired hands and drunks from town. Earl taunted back—frolicking with the Culbertson twins till his guardian came unglued, locking him out of his own house and praying loudly every night.

Earl spent his sixteenth winter alone in the barn with the flock. He felt martyred out in manger-land, and sipping heavily from the akvavit 'shine, Earl got himself confused to the edge of madness. All that seemed to help him cope was the uncomplicated gaze of one special ewe. An umber-coated Spael. No agenda in her emerald eyes, not a smidgen of superiority—always there with a nuzzle if needed and softer than anything God had ever made. Pure innocence, primal grace. Earl let his desire for being born of different skin, longing to wield a fabled tail, transgress the accepted mores of man and nature. Nothing about it felt wrong as it was happening, and the ungulate seemed to call his name in a vowelish moan. He could sense a rift in the order of things, that he was being granted a privileged view of some paradise. The soft metronome of pulse could be felt in the phantom length of his Harmony Arm as the ewe turned her sweet face toward him, ablink and cooing. Joy engulfed Earl in a beneficent flash, twice as bright as the infernal jolt that had taken his ma and pa. Some cosmic debt of amperage equalized.

When Earl was spent, she still squeezed tight. He'd heard the jokes—*those woolies'll lock up on you*—but never really believed this natural reflex. He was unable to free himself; all night long she clung. They drifted off in slumber, lost in the same forbidden dream.

His guardian lover came searching in the morning with an attorney, Melvin Fulton, in tow, ready to ship Earl off to boarding school. As Arthur had caught Guinevere and Lancelot, so these two beheld a sin so wrong it was burned indelible in both forever. Earl lay with the lamb he'd named Edith. His guardian, Lottie Poe, fell catatonic on the spot.

Edith was slaughtered with the rest of the flock, and Earl was sent away till, at eighteen, he returned to tend the family acres. He forswore alcohol and tried to bury the memory of what was done deeper than any grave—down below the aquifers, in a vein of salt, close enough to the core of the earth he hoped magma might boil it away. Never again raised large animals for commerce, only poultry, hare, and crops. Sometimes kept a horse or two. Earl withdrew from all but the most necessary social contact, and began a cruel self-damning penance—saltpetering himself daily to keep sirens from his loins, as well as devising masochistic rituals utilizing rusted agriculture equipment to assuage his shame.

Life marched on through seasons in passable existence till Earl was thirty-four, when Lottie escaped from the asylum up in Bigby and was found hanging above that very same spot in the barn. Lamb of God writ backwards in blood across her naked torso. Chester Fulton, Melvin's son, was sent out as the new County Assistant DA to adjudicate on what had happened. Ruled suicide officially, but his daddy had told him stories. Around Prairie Heights word spread, despite the vow to keep it mum. Wellington boots found hanging from Earl's powerline, his post office box stuffed with wool and condoms, *Hey Muttonfucker* scrawled on the side. Eventually those who knew of it died, moved on, or didn't care.

Earl gets the tail jar past the TSA, claiming it's a prize-winning *rakfisk*. The supervisor nibbles one of the "fermented fish" and nods approval. Crazy scandahoovians and their rancid food.

Vegas does indeed evoke Emerald City in the cab ride driving in—all agleam with neon promise against a burning western sky, the distant hills silhouetted like dead Lincoln lying there. Earl considers which of Dorothy's friends he might be, settling on Scarecrow, his innards being so weak, and him with so little education, though he wishes he were the Lion, cowardly or not.

The cab driver, a young double-amputee from Chad, victim of a warlord's "long sleeve" vengeance, tells Earl anything can happen here, proudly displaying new prosthetics he won the means for with a single spin at roulette.

"Art of the state!" he proclaims, with a blinding grin. Earl makes note of the cab number—nineteen—tipping the youth a crisp Uly, expertly snatched up between mechanical tongs.

Earl checks into the legendary Caesars Palace, one of the last standing vestiges of the old Strip. The staff sniffs him over—his snaggled teeth, what's left of them, rat-yellow from a life of chaw. Surely the man in front of them has not booked their third-best penthouse suite, The Diplomat, usually on reserve to comp *whales*—sheiks and hedge-fund scum, your sports MVPs and Russian oligarchs. All is quickly bona fide and Earl's mortified hands take the card key and the one USPS package waiting for his associate, Chester Fulton. The desk clerk recoils from the monstrous paws. Umpteen years of wrestling baling wire have forged a new map upon his palms, his broken fingers jut an awkward splay, poorly set by veterinarians. Earl is unable to form a fist with his left, but this does not mean he has no fight left within him. He's come here on a mission. It will take the Lion's courage, the passion of a reborn Tin Man, and all the stuffing he's got left. He's not here to beg some clever miracle—Earl's come to kill the damn Wizard.

The Strip is finally back to vice-as-usual after a half-baked Mumbai-style attack a few years ago during the poker tourneys at Binion's. Vegas had become half ghost town for a spell and ought not be looking down its snoot at anyone. It was never confirmed which affiliation was responsible, though several terror groups took credit. May as well have been operatives from Atlantic City or Pechanga as most every hotel on the Strip went bankrupt, and half remain kaput—dark, hulking mountains of dead neon and broken glass, encircled in razor wire. Steve Wynn had done a swan dive from the tower of the Bellagio, toupee flying, a Turner and Monet in his grip.

Earl stumbles off the elevator into his private wing, marveling at a gold-plated ice machine in the hallway. The suite is vast as a salt mine, the spectral hues of noble gases flashing everywhere outside the two-story windows. As Earl gives in to slumber, he ponders the fate of the other two packages.

Morning comes, and Earl wakes long before first light, as always. The displacing vastness of the room keeps him unsteady as he grabs a wastebasket, heading out in pj's to fetch more ice. Earl soaks in a tubful at some point nearly every night to numb the ungodly ache of his tumescence. As he stalks down the hall, he is aware that his ancient pajama material is worn to the nubbins, plastered with a repeating pattern of smiling sheep jumping over an irritated barnyard dog.

The cascading racket from the ice machine veils the steps of a dozen others coming down through a Restricted Roof Access door. When the machine cuts off, there are voices all around him. Without his bifocals, they are only shapes at first.

"Baaaaa," purrs a feminine voice close to his ear, and as he turns—a tall black lamb runs the soft tip of a rubber hoof across the pajama cloth, then baaaas again. "Got to love the kitschy threads. You must be the oldest little boy in the whole wide world," she speaks with coquettish flair, a hint of east Euro accent.

Earl blushes, turning to behold a group of bright creatures in weak focus, rubbing his eyes to dispel this residue of dream—but they remain. Surely these are people, walking upright, except an oinking Swedish Landrace crawling on all fours with a collar round its neck, tethered up in the hand of a latex Leopard.

"Orwell," says Lamb.

"Beg pardon?" Earl asks.

"You're supposed to know to ask it—not divulge it to a perfect stranger!" barks a five-foot beaver next to her.

"Orwell?" Earl asks.

"He *is* perfect. And he just said it—it's been said," Lamb pout-tongues the beaver back.

As a Bengal tiger and a Hereford, a gray wolf, poodle, billy goat and bear skip off together with a llama and kangaroo, Black Lamb places a magenta card in Earl's gnarled fingers, then hurries to catch up with the menagerie, shouting back over her shoulder, "Password of the day!"

Earl follows after them like a child as they stuff every cubic inch of his elevator—an Otis ark of colorful fur waving back at him. The green-eyed Lamb meets his gaze as the door slowly closes.

Earl looks down—finds himself aroused. He's been off his saltpeter a month now, and purple urges course shamefully through him as he examines the card. *Tonight's Theme: Frisky Business!!! Cuddle Up—Room 305—Circus Circus 11 pm. Best Soiree at Plushapalooza.*

At the desk downstairs, Earl tells of the strangeness he's seen as two concierges examine a torn section of wet synthetic pelt dangling from a door hinge.

"Dammit Jerry—they got up on the roof again."

"Ziffy fucking pervs—been photo-bombing the whole town last two days. Instagramming the *Kama Sutra,* no doubt. Remember FurFest two years ago?"

To Earl, these rude employees may as well speak Mandarin. After buying a toothbrush, he ventures to the roof himself, stopping half-way up the stairs, his one lung burning, heart a piledriver in his chest.

Up top he takes in the view—Oz as Oz could ever be in the early desert light. Earl finds scattered photos, discarded shots of poor focus and frame. The huge stuffed critters blurred in graphic images, humping and groping one another with a neon landscape behind them. In one, Black Lamb sandwiched between Bear and Bengal. Earl looks around, then secures them in his pocket.

He wanders over to an expansive skylight, peering down into a boardroom being set up for a meeting, a banner draped above a huge ironwood table: The Future of Food Week. Welcome Sauget-Prochem Industries. Earl's Viking brain begins a slow percolation. His vague plan as a stockholder (five thousand shares given in transaction) is to arrive early for the conclave in the main ballroom the day after tomorrow, wait for the right moment to make a move toward the Board on the dais, a corset of Beaver Brand around him. Somehow get someone to answer to him. But now a better scenario occurs to Earl—the worst of the worst will be here, huddling giddy with their secrets, tallying up their lucre. Why endanger others needlessly, average Joes and pensioned grannies. Tomorrow or the next day, after he's spent himself on a last bender, he'll make a stand, if he can only get his blood up to go through with it.

Earl sleeps away the day, then goes for a walk down the Strip at dusk, dazzled by the vanity of scale and garish light. Hearing a major ruckus inside the lobby of Slots of Fun, he watches as more of the large personified creatures romp across tabletops, chased by security, tossing chips in the air to frenzy the crowd and make their getaway. He follows the pack of furries as they stampede down the street into more casinos. These beasts have cast enchantment upon him, and if curiosity wishes him dead—so be it.

In the window of a metal box on the curb, a headline and photo catch his eye—Explosion at Denver Sorting Facility. Postal Terror Suspect in Custody. Chester Fulton's meaty paw trying to block his mug from a paparazzi flash.

"They call it comeuppance," Earl whispers to himself, then horks up a mad-ass bellow of laughter.

Several paces back, Black Lamb is keeping Earl in her sights, walking with Beaver and Kangaroo, following wherever he might go. They watch as Earl gambles away half the Ulys in his roll. Five-thousand-dollar bets at roulette. Same number every time. Black 19. He keeps enough to try again later, laughing his way across the street, then stops to gaze upon the endless line at Bob Stupak Jr's All You Can Eat Gourmand Buffet, where corpulent humapotamus families stack gravy and pizza upon mac & cheese on top of chicken-fried everything.

How many even know what hunger is today? Or real food? Earl reckons that evolution surely ceased with the landing on the moon, then went into retrograde. There will be tough times ahead, for certain, and the mindless herds have no idea of the hardships to come—nor the vaguest clue of ones that went before them.

In 1838 a clan of seven Brothers Gunderson and families of a dozen cousins and friends embarked from Hannibal for the free homesteading in the West. By '42, three years into absolute drought, famine had whittled two hundred down to sixty.

Passing scouts of the Ponca Tribe left pemmican and bison stew for these *walking ghosts*. The few remaining livestock were slaughtered to make it through one last winter—their entire food stock mixed with milk, blood, and bonemeal into a great frozen ball of ice left near the door of the sod lodge, away from the pitiful hearth. Each Gunderson was allowed ten quick licks upon waking and ten more before bed.

Every root was torn from the cracked earth with the spring thaw. In fall they'd lived off horseflies and skeeters trapped with honeyed bunting, but come April even the flying vermin had not returned. All dug for tiny wriggling things deep in the parched ground till finger bones were showing. Clay became a staple. Inedible jimson weed and a well gone saline drove half of them to madness.

In delirium, some began to nurse from others' veins. Before the "law of the sea" became acceptable on this cursed dry land, elders made plans for a last meal of lead. Ammo was one thing they still had aplenty.

All gathered above the dry creek gully, but just before the final deed commenced, a cloud appeared on the far east horizon, racing toward them like a great spearhead, dark and churning, surely fat with rain. As it began to blot the day, it then seemed only some torrent of smoke from a distant fire, as what looked like huge shards of ash began to fall around them. The next moment these were revealed instead to be dying birds, not embers—plummeting from an impossible flock above. A mass migration of passenger pigeons, a billion in number, blackened the sky for the next six hours. It took that long for the flock to pass over while every living Gunderson fired skyward until the last bullet was spent. A haystack of lean fowl was collected, taller than a man, wide as a barn. Avian throats were slit and wounds squeezed empty, the precious crimson trickle bottled in preserve jars. Organ meat was salted, dried for harsh tomorrows, feathers stripped for bedding. A feast was had like none before or since. Six of the Gunderson clan died of gorging, their atrophied gullets clogged as surely as if they'd consumed Solomon's mortar.

Rain fell unceasing the next year and the year after, washing away every soddy they'd ever built, but filling aquifers again. Though the passenger pigeon went extinct in the early twentieth century, an unbroken chain of Gundersons lived on upon the land—till Earl signed it all away with the stroke of a pen.

At the door of the Vista Room, third floor of Circus Circus, Earl whispers "Orwell" and is welcomed in through a purple curtain. A few dozen vendors sell items for the fur-fiend clientele. He passes tables and stalls displaying exotic polyester pelts, massive heads, and decorative tails. His belly tingles from these alluring sights as an old Die Antwoord tune pulses—*I fink u freeky and I like you a lot*. The magnetism that drew him here is a vexing thing. Earl did not actually decide to come; his feet just brought him, as if there were no other choice.

Black Lamb steals up behind Earl and baaaaas hello again. He turns, with youthful delight, looking her up and down, then quickly glances away at the scene around him, shaking his head.

"Tryin' to get my mind around this all."

"Simple really—our souls are animal, our poor flesh born sadly human."

Lamb leads him on a tour, nodding to mascot beings and living toys; all seem to know her well. She outs a few of the semifamous beneath their fur—a federal judge, a southpaw reliever for the Orioles, two members of the Belgian royal line.

"Some of us just play cards. Like those posters of poker dogs. Or take in the sights together. A show maybe. But come the witching hour—a certain portion invariably jumps in the pile."

Earl thinks she must be able to hear the aberrant notions swirling in his head, that she is some sorceress able to gaze deep into his sordid past.

"We're full-spectrum here—het, gay, bi, asexual—we put gender in the blender. Faux fur only, unless like mine—something normally shorn. It's Rambouillet fleece by the way," she tells Earl, encouraging him to stroke it, "dyed with squid juice. No true zoo ever! Nothing torn from things we love and wanna be. Strictly verboten. No endangered pelts or taxi'd cocks—go to Puyallup or Berlin you want that heinous shit."

Again, as if it's Mandarin, Earl can only nod to the gibberish.

"What's your name, kind sir?"

"Chester Fulton," Earl says. "And yours?"

"What would you like it to be?"

He stammers, eyes turned down to his feet. "Edith. Would that be all right?"

"Almost no one's an Edith anymore. A good name—Edith."

"Yes, it is," Earl says, raising his gaze to meet hers.

Earl tries on a sheep outfit, but realizes he is on the wrong side of the wool. He was always predator in randy dreams, never prey, and is lucky to get the last red fox costume at the event. Black Lamb helps him dress, but thinks it way too clean, wants Earl to roll around a bit in the loam a backhoe has unearthed in the parking lot out back. She would like him wild and ripe.

Earl scoops up a handful, measures it by smell and feel. Tastes just a smidgeon, then lets the particles fly off in the wind.

"Dead earth. Landfill—just dust of city crap."

Instead, he rolls in a mulching pile of chestnut leaves, and though it greatly pains his tumescence, Earl finds it soothing to be bossed by sassy Lamb.

"Again, again Little Fox—back the other way now. Oh, what a mess you've made of your beautiful fur!"

Up in the Vista Room, Edith offers medication for his agony. Earl shows her a bag of his own with hundreds of such pills, plus a dozen never-filled prescriptions. He generally prefers to endure what's ailing, unless he cannot sleep. She pops a few like candy, then grabs the bulk of the lot, returning in a few minutes.

"And change." Edith hands him a wad of cash, then dramatically displays a well-worn lion suit she's procured.

"Try this one, sire—much more kingly." She bows to him.

The costume is, if not in fact Bert Lahr's from the original *Wizard of Oz*, a perfect, aged replica.

"Was up for auction tomorrow, but I preempted. Broker's a Continhead."

Earl beholds his metamorphosis in a full-length mirror. He beams at the sight of the mechanical tail that seems to have a mind of its own. Harmonic appendage indeed.

Earl picks up the whole tab for a lavish Thai dinner before the "Cuddle Up." All creatures raise a glass to Lion. The outfit had been previously owned by one Jimbo Nailor, who died last month. Many have not heard of his passing, so Earl is in constant bombardment of "Hey Jimbo—how's the actuary business?" and "Give my best to Doris." Jimbo this and Jimbo that. After trying to explain a few times, Earl just goes along. Why not be him? Or Chester? Why not make things easier?

It is here—everyone's eyes lost in a world of pretend pelt—that Earl finally understands what being social means. He is no longer a lonely dying farmer too proud to utter a word about it. He is a special beast among special beasts—it is a beastly heaven. The mission on his mind recedes. Why not live among these strange folk while he can? Leave the Gunderson name unsullied. Earl is free to do anything he wishes now. No fusarium head blight and crown gall to attend to. It matters not if it ever rains. The day and night are both his to squander.

Earl sits for a photo op with Flying Monkey, watching his little lamb work the room, cavorting with creatures both humble and grand. A few are making hand-painted signs for an upcoming protest against SPI, but just as many seem apolitical, here for taboo only.

Edith slips off to the kitchen to meet with Beaver, who pulls a yellow-and-black-ringed outfit from a case, then peels off his fur, naked for a moment, quickly dressing up again as plump Bumble Bee.

"Got a whole hive of the reals to set loose too," he tells her.

Earl creeps closer, like a big cat on the savanna, near enough to hear Edith's hushed voice amid the hubbub.

"Working this sweet ole geeze. Big stockholder, I think. Maybe even on the Board. Has the predilections. Trying to swing us getting up in that high-roller suite. We use the ventilation ducts—let the hive have their way with those SPI honchos down in the boardroom."

"Ray Burdock has two GoPros," Beaver says. "Taffy Lindhorn can link it up. We beam *Bee's Revenge* live! A thousand stings—a million hits in no time."

Earl hears their agenda and does not care. Doesn't even mind when Edith slips a few knock-out drops in the stiff drink she hands him. As the world begins to fade, Earl leans to whisper. "What's up your sleeve? Same notion's me—so's you know."

Black Lamb, uncertain of the context of her lion's slurred comment, shrugs it off as only a sex wish.

"I know, honey. I know."

Earl swoons, a rare smile on his lips as he slumps to the floor.

Kangaroo shushes the crowd and announces that the Vegas Police are downstairs, ready to bust everyone. Repercussions from all the frolicking on the Strip. Edith tells the gathered zoo that Jimbo—the Courageous Lion—has offered up his whale suite but only if they can all be highly discreet.

"Grab your go bags, dress back down to street clothes, take the western fire escape. Meet up at Caesars—three at a time—private elevator number five in the Baccarat Room. We should be good till maid service."

A chant begins: "Jimbo saves the day! Jimbo saves the day!"

Sometime after midnight, Earl rouses in his vast suite, now filled with dozens of faux mammals, a few cuddly reptiles, and a huge bird or two. Some watch *Where the Wild Things Are* on the eighty-inch Samsung, while others play board games, sipping beverages and chatting as if at a garden-variety garden party. But in the darkened half of the suite, there is something else afoot.

Earl stands, wobbly, still fuddled, loins with a mind of their own—what she slipped him, some powerful lusting agent as well. K or E or X, Y, Z. He is drawn to the myriad hues of softness rippling in the half-light; the barnyard moans.

Edith sees him at the edge of the *pile* that spills from a circular red satin bed. Hoofs, paws, and other tender appendages—an anemone of welcome—pull him down into the thick of the writhing. The smell of fuck. Of sweat and sad mildew. Willpower erodes, and a carnal mew grows to full alpha roar as Earl gives in to outré urges. His and theirs. The throbbing collective desire.

Earl had known a woman. He had loved a lamb. Now he lies with a chimera of the two. A kaleidoscope undulates in the ceiling mirror above. Pain subsides as pleasure crests, and Earl falls from consciousness once more.

\* \* \*

As always, he wakes before the sun. Flesh aflame and crying for opiation. He extracts himself from the snoring *menagerie à trois douzaines* and finds Edith—headless now—in the master bathroom, in cahoots with Beaver again. A human face, forty, perhaps fifty, and still stunning, staring at him with the same green eyes of his lamb.

"Some fun, huh, Chester? Never again like the first time though."

"Weren't my first."

"You're a good man. I know you are," she scoffs, doubting him, "so I think I'll clue you in—"

"Don't. Just don't," says Beaver, clad halfway in the bee suit again. Earl steps over, towering above him.

"Get yourself back out of that," he orders, looking to Edith, who nods. Earl can barely keep standing as he begins to disrobe and balks at stripping off the bottom half—wishing to keep his mechanical tail. Earl's alabaster torso is arrayed with dozens of protruding masses.

"Benign?"

Earl shakes his head. "It's got me in the vise." Edith leans in and kisses a cancerous bulge. He trembles, rendered boyish again from such a delicate gesture.

"Heights gimme the willies sometimes. Could use a hand up there," Earl says. He produces the mailed package and begins to slather Beaver Brand goo all over his dying skin.

Back in full pelt, Beaver puts a Camel in his lips and pulls a lighter. Earl skewers him with that thousand-yard stare.

"Not 'less you wanna meet your maker."

"Well, maybe I do. Just might tell him what a royal fuck-up he is."

"Go on, then—flint up and take us with you. Got plenty to ask the dumb bastard myself."

The Beaver backs down, giving up a smile, then a laugh, infecting Earl and Edith too—growing loud enough to wake some others. The two help pull the insect outfit flush, metamorphosing Earl into a fine bumble bee above, yet still a jungle king below. They watch as Earl gently straps the sticks of vintage TNT around his waist, lacing wires carefully to a makeshift detonator secured by a thumb gadget.

"This is what we are? The Terror? We've become them now?" asks Beaver as Earl pulls on the bee's head, antennae boinking in jumpy spirals.

"This is just for show, yes, Chester? Couldn't really go off?" Edith asks.

"Odds are agin' it."

"Then why?"

"You wanted 'em stung. Shake things up for a day. I got a score to settle. Need an answer I never got. A why. No writ or lackey with a bribe'll do. It'll likely get me shot, but some fool's gonna answer for what they done."

Earl prepares two huge horse syringes, filling one with the pickled elixir from his tail jar, the other with a pure dose of Sauget-Prochem Industries' ubiquitous herbicide: Stampede.

"Everybody here—get 'em gone," Earl tells them. "Hit the road and don't look back. Solitary thing I gotta do. Justified. But still a wicked deed."

Earl corks the needle tips, slipping both carefully back into buckskin holsters he straps to his waist.

"And so's you know—I'm not a Chester any more'n I'm a Jimbo. They'll know that soon. I'm a Gunderson. Which one don't matter. You can tell them reporters—I was every last one of 'em."

The antennae cease wobbling for a moment. Edith taps them—they go circling madly once more, in sync with the tail and its curious meandering around his girth.

Bees begin to stir as a shaft of light hits a plastic box and warms the hive.

"What about them?" Beaver asks. "We have two confederates in the food-service crew. They're putting superglue in the locks once we start piping the bugs in."

Earl horks up another mad-ass bellow of laughter. "The time is nigh."

On the roof, the three creatures see an angry anvil off in the western sky, the horizon rolled up like a rug and heading their way. A massive, looming dust storm.

"All but my folks set off the land come the dust bowl," Earl tells them. "They'd get those cruel blankets of earth shaking out every other week."

There is a long dead pause as Earl takes a deep breath, tries to accustom himself to the height. The board members file in below, peeling off their Armani and ties, the room uncomfortable with the air conditioning shut off ahead of the storm. Earl reaches out to touch the glass. Feels the warmth of the windowpane. Lightning flickers in the distance. A tempest took Earl's folks away. Maybe their spirits come now, in the sands of this one—returning to take him with them.

A clot of pigeons flutters near; one alights on Earl's shoulder, and he takes it as an omen.

"Ever hear tell of the passenger pigeon?" Earl asks.

"Like on Brooklyn rooftops in the movies?" asks Beaver, but Earl shakes his head.

"'Nother species. Those are messengers. The passengers—long gone. Meant more'n you'd ever know to us Gundersons. Salvation. There were once as many as stars in the sky. The very last one, named Martha, died in captivity at the Cincinnati Zoo. September 1, 1914."

"The day St. Petersburg was renamed Petrograd," Edith adds, a greater hint of Belarusian accent on display. "Your Edith is Olga, by the way."

"Dominic," Beaver nods. "Québécois."

Earl sighs, his stoic nature melting loquacious, time being at a premium with too many words left unsaid.

"My pa Olaf, when he was a boy, saw that bird its last day on this earth. Granddaddy drove twelve hundred miles just to give thanks. Pa met a little girl there. Few years older'n him. They sat around from opening till closing. Didn't see any other animals. Just watched that common dirty bird tryin' to flap its wings. Lost half its beak somehow, couldn't eat no more—wheezin' away, tryin' to hold on. The flesh just keeps atryin'. Another breath'll save you—you just get to the next."

Beaver works a glass cutter with a suction and a handle, making a large circle in the surface of a four-foot panel. As he removes it, the glass slips and shatters on the roof.

"The wheezes they slowed. More each time. Flesh finally knew. There's another clock we got. Inside all o' us, you listen deep. It's there. We got a compass too we never use. A tail that should have been. A third eye."

Beaver scrolls a list on his iWatch readout, hits *play*, and Arcade Fire's "My Body Is a Cage" shimmers out from his wearable speakers.

"They held a memorial. That little girl and my daddy. Together they wrote the sweetest eulogy, as only kids can do. Kept writing back and forth to each other till they was of age. Then he sent for her."

An aquifer of tears flows full-on from Earl now. Years pent up inside him. "Didn't have me till in their forties. Hard to get my seed to plant, I guess. Left me brotherless. Sisterless too. Blessing maybe. No one left to shame."

"You hear yours now, don't you, Earl? That soft clock ticking."

He scrunches his Shar-Pei brow. How'd she know his name?

"No worries. You're our hero—Gary Cooper in *High Noon*."

Earl spews his last tobacky rainbow through the hole in the glass—it splats softly down below, drooling an artful pattern across the poached salmon set out for brunch.

"Always partial to *Shane* myself," he says, freeing a few bees before Beaver begins to pump the hive into the AC system. Earl shakes and makes them sting him. They seem to sense where his cancer bulges out, picking those spots to poke with their lances. Pain melts sublime again.

Beaver affixes a tiny GoPro to Earl's striped head, then sets another to gaze down from the hole of removed glass, along with a microphone and transponder. Bees begin to sting the Board below, who, attempting to flee, find the doors locked. Lamb and Beaver both kiss Earl farewell.

Earl saddles himself up over the rail, tearing his outfit on the edge of the broken glass as he lowers himself with a tied-off rope. Blood drizzles down, spotting paperwork on the table. As he descends, Earl can see a security guard walkie someone about the insect menace.

A wave of vertigo cascades through him, and Earl slips from the rope—plunging thirty feet—hitting hard, facedown. Several bones shatter in the fall. At first, most all in the room are only concerned that someone could be hurt.

"We got an injured protester in some animal getup," radios security, but rolling him over, they all see the bomb—Earl's thumb on the trigger. Security starts for a gun. Earl shakes his head.

"Your piece on the table. Now. That walkie too."

"Code ten. Zeke Alpha out," security whispers before obeying Earl's command. The Board is frozen, waiting for someone to do something, the only sounds nervous breath, hand-swats, and a din of buzzing. Earl looks up at the hole in the glass, sees Black Lamb and Beaver wave goodbye, leaving the wearable speakers and iWatch, which begin to play Antony and the Johnsons' cover of "Knockin' on Heaven's Door." Cranked loud.

"Had a lot to say. But it don't matter. Not gonna change you people an iota."

Murmurs exchanged about what's leaking from him.

"This ain't honey you—you fuckers," Earl whispers, convulsing from his mortal wounds, then tries to shake it off and sit up.

"Who can tell me who ruled on taking the Gunderson platte? Twenty-five hundred shit acres in Fenton County outside Prairie Heights? One o' your test farms now. You stole it from my family. Hundred eighty-five years we lived and died there."

Nothing but headshakes and silence.

"Then everybody pays the price, I guess."

Panic begins anew as an elegant, silver-coiffed woman pulls a Taser from her purse, holding it between her legs.

"Okay—maybe I just take one o' you. Fair is fair. But you all decide who it'll be. You can remember the cowardly sin for the rest of your days."

The collective angst subsides a bit in knowing most of them may live, that the filthy, broken man bleeding out on their ironwood table can be reasoned with.

Earl coughs up a splash of blackened blood across the white-fish platter. "Nature—she's hard enough. So don't fuck with her any more'n you got to. Go back to what you were good at. You made a fine poison."

The faces of the Board were of varied shape and symmetry. Deep-set eyes and bulging thyroid ones. Some brown, but mainly blue. Complexions generally of fair pallor, but not all. Mostly men, but not all. Age skewed high as might any body of the corporate elite. Who they were—their names, titles, and appearances—was not important. Nor their lives and lineage. They sold their souls and were better off forgotten. The words they said in selfish pleading were not worth noting, as they barely hesitated forming consensus on one of their own to sacrifice. The youngest member of the cabal. The swarthiest too. He'd been willed his numerous shares and had been an irritant voice of change, trying to turn the moral ship around. The young man emptied his bladder and voided his bowels even before Earl ordered the CEO to jab the tip of each horse syringe deep into his arms. The ash-templed honcho did so without hesitation. The others, in surprisingly orderly fashion, fell into line, taking turns—each pushing the plungers in a notch. Not too little, not too much. All the same incremental bit. Complicit, perhaps, but, legally innocent they conjectured, since no individual's action alone was sufficient to cause death, and all was done under duress.

Earl lifted his head a bit, tilting the camera to witness, bee antennae wiggling through the frame. The camera mounted far above looked down as if it were a deadbeat God finally checking in on his abandoned brood. Both transmitted to the jaded world. The board member quivered near death, and most tried to look away, but Earl ordered them to view it to the end as someone on the other side of the door blowtorched his way through the lock.

"You watch him die! Then you can all go have a great Fourth of July," he promised.

Once the young man passed, Earl gave the signal, that he was removing his thumb from the detonator, freeing these shit weasels to wreak their havoc upon the earth once more. The Board lined up against the wall as Earl rolled all the way over, staring up.

The first Vegas SWAT member through the door was itchy—saw Earl's elbow ease to the table surface and fired off a warning shot. It ricocheted around the room and gut-shot the CEO. The commander told them all to hold steady. Everyone froze for the longest time. In the angled square of light above, Earl saw the dark clouds pass into view. The silver-coiffed woman inched her zapper up over the edge of the table, ready for a hero move.

"No—God—no!" screamed someone as she activated the power.

Earl's errant tail rose like a riled cobra. A mind of its own. The SWAT team took it for a threat. Or an excuse. As they always do. They could shoot legs or arms or anywhere, but a dark logic insisted on the kill. A headshot would have ended it, but the novice had gone for the heart—the bleeding honey drip of Beaver Brand trembling with each beat.

The plume from the explosion had roiled high with golden fire, shapeshifting as fierce air rushed in ahead of the dust storm. Some had seen pareidoliac shapes within it, even an animal totem or two. Black Lamb, Beaver and the others, dressed normal again, had watched it meet the great dust wall, eaten quickly by the greater prey, melting into angry sky. All took shelter inside the boarded ruins of Binion's as the sand was quickly upon the town. Every molecule of Earl, of all in the boardroom, was lost within it.

They say the western front rode hard that day, that the explosion had been drafted all the way up into the jet stream—particles of Earl had perhaps found their way back to those forsaken Gunderson acres. To the Little Anvil outside Prairie Heights.

Only the wind knows for sure.

# ACKNOWLEDGMENTS

I would like to particularly thank:

Jim Krusoe, who gave me the prompt, "Write about a man in a room with a plant," which begat "Rubiaux Rising," the first story I sent out into the world. Jim has been a continuing mentor for me at his three-decades-long Wednesday night class at Santa Monica College that I still attend time to time.

Andrew Tonkovich, *Santa Monica Review* editor, who published "Rubiaux" (and other stories) and described my excessive style as "starting over the top, then somehow topping that."

And most especially Heidi Pitlor, who plucked "RR" from the stack, and Alice Sebold, for the unbelievable gift of choosing it for inclusion in *The Best American Short Stories 2009*, thus enabling me to believe this fiction thing was really possible. (The latter also encouraged me to embrace my "overt" style.)

All my Antioch Los Angeles Creative Writing MFA mentors and workshop leaders: Steve Heller, Brad Kessler, Rob Roberge, Susan Taylor Chehak, Jim Krusoe, Dodie Bellamy, Tara Ison, and Leonard Chang (and a ton of fellow Purple Martin students and those of other cohorts there).

Julie Stern, who worked with me closely on several stories.

Michael Griffith and Nicola Mason at *Cincinnati Review*, who published multiple stories, and Nicola for superb edits to improve previously published versions for Acre Books.

Stephen Donadio, who declared I had "unfettered imagination" (and that was a good thing), and Carolyn Kuebler, my editors at *New England Review* who also published multiple stories. Along with Marcia Pomerance and Janice Obuchowski at NER.

The Sewanee Writers' Conference for bestowing a Tennessee Williams Scholarship (workshop leaders Steve Yarbrough and Jill McCorkle) and Bread Loaf Writers' Conference for their Scholarship (and workshop leader Antonya Nelson).

Other anthology editors and guest editors: Jason Lee Brown and Shanie Latham at *New Stories from the Midwest,* along with Guest Editors Rosellen Brown (2013) and Antonya Nelson (2018). Also editor Francesca Lia Block for her anthology *Love Magick* and her notes on other stories.

Other editors: Katya Apekina, Steve Weddle, Vern Miller, Marge Piercy, Joanna Beth Tweedy, and Barry Kitterman.

The feedback of Dzanc Creative Writing Sessions: Gina Frangello, John Domini, Kyle Minor, Alissa Nutting, and George Singleton (also Dzanc honchos Dan Wickett and Steve Gillis).

Other readers and supporters: Antonia Crane, Flavia Loeb, Glen Pitre, Gretchen Somerfeld, Marsha Kinder, Dawna Kemper, Julie Cline, O-Lan Jones, Stephen Day, Sandy Yang, Jennifer Genest, Mark Maynard, Diane Gurman, Matthew Specktor, Andrea Pappas, The 30b gang, Emily Schultz, Brian Davis, Nina Buckless, Christina Lynch, Phyllis Murphy, Christine Sneed, Elizabeth McKenzie, Ed Park, Kerry Slattery, Ken Wheat, Alan Heathcock, Jenny Burman, Victoria Patterson, Stefan Kiesbye, Paul Chadwick, Edan Lepucki, Jeff Fiskin, Wendy Ortiz, Renée Zuckerbrot, Will Boast, Peg Alford Pursell, Lou Mathews, Jim Ruland, Sally Shore, Susan Hayden, Eugene Cross, Edward Bunker, Sheila Bender, Howard Rodman, Jillian Lauren, Sam Ligon, Richard Barron, Jane Jenkins, Steve Erickson (and plenty more who've slipped my mind).

The stories herein initially appeared, sometimes in altered form, in *Cincinnati Review* ("Mulligan," "Harmony Arm"), *Fifth Wednesday* ("Woonsocket"), *Meridian* ("Escharotomy"), *Missouri Review* ("Eggtooth"; audio contest winner), *New England Review* ("Her Great Blue," "Wraiths in Swelter"), *Santa Monica Review* ("Rubiaux Rising," "Chronicles of an Umbra Hound"), *Quiddity* ("Blood Up"), and *Zone 3* ("Exit Left"). "Rubiaux Rising" was reprinted in *Best American Short Stories*, 2009, and "Mulligan" and "Wraiths in Swelter" in *New Stories from the Midwest* (2013, 2018).